Maddy Alone

Pamela Brown

Longwater Books

First published in Great Britain in 1945
Thomas Nelson & Sons Ltd

This paperback edition published in Great Britain in 2007 by Longwater Books.

ISBN-13: 978-0-9552428-1-6

Typeset in 11/14pt Monotype Calisto

Illustration by Lucy Davey

Printed and bound in Great Britain by Antony Rowe Ltd, Chippenham, Wiltshire

Longwater Books
4 Park View
Lower Road
Erlestoke
Devizes
Wiltshire SN10 5UE
UK

About the author

Pamela Brown was born in 1924 and wrote her best-known novel, *The Swish of the Curtain*, when she was 14. She sent the manuscript to the book's first publishers, Thomas Nelson, in the early days of the Second World War. Nelson's offices were bombed in the Blitz, but the manuscript was saved, although the publishers had no contact details for the author. She wrote to them a year later and received a reply saying they would publish the book, which they did in 1941. Four sequels followed, the first of which was *Maddy Alone*.

Pamela Brown trained at RADA, and worked as a professional actress. She subsequently worked as a radio and television producer, but continued to write for children, publishing books until the 1980s. Pamela Brown died in 1989.

Notes about the setting

Maddy Alone was first published in the 1940s, and the following references may require some additional explanation for the modern reader.

Before decimalisation in 1969, British currency consisted of pounds, shillings and pence:
12 pence = 1 shilling
20 shillings = 1 pound
21 shillings = 1 guinea
so *three and six* means "three shillings and sixpence".

Deanna Durbin and Shirley Temple were popular child film stars of the time.

Lyons Corner Houses were a chain of restaurants.

The School Certificate was a school exam taken at age 16. It was replaced in 1951 by O-levels. O-levels were replaced by GCSEs in 1988.

MADDY REBELS

Maddy woke up, remembered it was arithmetic this morning, and flung her teddy bear out of the bed on to the floor. Then she turned over and went to sleep again.

"Maddy! Get up! You're late already and your breakfast is getting cold," Mrs. Fayne shouted up the stairs for the third time that morning.

"I *am* getting up." Maddy pulled the eiderdown over her head, feeling as bad-tempered as an advertisement of night starvation. The thought of her unfinished homework was a weight on her mind, and there was something else – something worse – what was it? Sleepily her thoughts groped for it – Oh, of course! The holidays. The others weren't coming home. Sandra, her elder sister had gone to Dramatic School together with their next-door neighbours, the Halfords, Nigel, Bulldog, and Vicky, and Lynette and Jeremy Darwin. Maddy, being too young, was left at home to continue her schooling. For weeks she had looked forward to their return for the Easter holidays, then yesterday she had received a letter from Sandra to say that she was the only one coming. The others were all wanted for a holiday show that their academy were giving.

Maddy went over in her mind all the preparations she had made for their coming; how she had scrubbed out the Blue Door Theatre, the disused chapel where they used to give their shows; her efforts to renovate all the costumes in the wardrobe; her searchings in Fenchester Public Library for suitable plays. And now they were not coming. All that lay ahead was examinations and then the blankness of the holidays. For the hundredth time Maddy thought, "Oh, *why* am I only twelve? Why do the others always do all the exciting things before me?"

The sound of her mother's feet on the stairs made her leap out of bed and into the bathroom for a "lick and a promise". As she dressed she muttered, "Horrid old tunic – Beastly old stockings –" and made an extremely ugly face at herself in the glass as she tied up the stumps of her yellow pigtails.

Mrs. Fayne sighed as Maddy banged the dining-room door on entering. "Oh, here you are at last. I thought you must have got sleeping sickness."

"Wish I had," growled Maddy.

"Now don't be naughty, Maddy dear. Do hurry up and eat your breakfast. Did you do your arithmetic eventually last night?"

"No, Mummy."

"But won't you get into trouble?"

"Yes, Mummy."

"I really don't know what's come over you since the others went away. I've never seen you so bad-tempered. You really must pull yourself together. Whatever will Sandra think of you?"

Maddy drew patterns in her porridge. "I don't care what she thinks."

"Really, Maddy, I despair of you. I shall tell your father what a naughty girl you're being." Mrs. Fayne's tone was sharp.

"And what could he do about it?"

"He could stop your pocket-money and then you wouldn't waste it on going to the cinema all the time."

Maddy dropped her spoon. "But it's Deanna Durbin's new film next week. Oh, Mummy, you are horrid. You know I want to see it."

"Well, you'll have to improve a lot if you're to be allowed to go," said Mrs. Fayne firmly. "The first thing to be done is that arithmetic!" She handed Maddy a copy of *Simple Arithmetical Problems*. "Are these the ones?"

"Yes. But it's no good. I can't do them."

"You can if you try. Now here we are. Listen. It's quite easy. 'If three men, A, B, and C, have to dig a field one acre in size, and A does one-twelfth, and B does eight-fifteenths, what does C do?'"

"Goes on strike, I should think," Maddy growled into her grapefruit.

"Oh, Maddy, dear, please try to concentrate," pleaded Mrs. Fayne. "That's not funny. No wonder all your teachers complain about you."

"Some of them quite like me," said Maddy complacently.

"They wouldn't if they saw you at home. I sometimes wish you had gone away with the others."

Maddy jumped from the table. "*You* wish I had! How do you think *I* feel about it? Here I am learning about horrible men digging beastly fields when Sandra and all the others are learning the things I want to know. I'm not interested in fields, or digging, or arithmetic, or algebra, or geometry, or spelling, or anything they teach me at school. I'm wasting my time – that's what I'm doing – I'm wasting the best years of my life. Youth is passing me by while I sit at a desk wearing a stuffy gym tunic –" She burst into tears of self-pity. "Well, I'm not going to any longer! So there! I'm not even going to school any more and you can't make me, and if you try to I shall do something terrible, so that you'll be sorry for ever after!"

"Maddy! How can you be so naughty!" exclaimed Mrs. Fayne.

Tears rolled down Maddy's face unchecked. "I'm *not* naughty! I'm not naughty!" she screamed, "I'm just unhappy and nobody cares. You don't care, nor does Daddy, or Sandra, or Jeremy, or Nigel, or anyone, not even the Bishop –" At the thought of the Bishop's apparent desertion of her since the others left, she wept even more bitterly.

"And what would the Bishop say if he were to see you now?" demanded her mother. "He'd be sorry he ever let you play in the Blue Door Theatre and took you to Stratford-on-Avon. In fact, if I see the Bishop in the town this morning I shall tell him what a wicked girl you're being."

Maddy gasped. "Oh, Mummy! You *couldn't* do that –"

"I most certainly shall."

Maddy's tears burst out afresh. "I shall never forgive you if you do. I'll – I'll go upstairs and lock myself in my room and I won't come out until you promise not to tell the Bishop about me."

Mrs. Fayne assumed nonchalance. "I'm sure I don't care *how* long you stay there. You'll get into trouble for not going to school this morning, but I know you'll come down when you're hungry."

"I shan't!" shouted Maddy, "I'll starve and then you'll be sorry –"

"Oh no, I shan't," her mother told her airily, "I should be quite pleased if you lost a little puppy fat."

Maddy ran upstairs to her room shouting, "Oh, you're horrid – you're horrid – and I won't ever come down from my room – Never –" She flung herself on the bed until her sobs subsided and then began to reflect what a nuisance being naughty was. She didn't really enjoy crying and being difficult, but sometimes it was so necessary. She stared hopelessly round the room, picked up her teddy bear and dried her eyes on him. What on earth was she going to do now? Going to school this morning was out of the question, but there would certainly be trouble when she did go – and then there was the question of lunch-time. The only refreshment her bedroom offered was on the mantlepiece – a tin of cough sweets that made one sick after eating too many. The possibilities of a siege were not very promising. Her eye fell on a copy of *Modern One-Act Plays*. She was half-way through one about Mary Queen of Scots. She picked up the book and was soon immersed. The tears dried on her cheeks.

Mrs. Fayne set off to do her shopping with a heavy heart. So Maddy was being difficult again. Secretly she was sorry for her. It was only natural that she should miss the other six children after the exciting times they had had over the Blue Door Theatre. But these tantrums were impossible and must not go on. In the distance she saw a familiar figure approaching. The large black hat – the thin gaitered legs – yes, it was the Bishop, seraphic of countenance as ever. His lean face brightened as he recognised her.

"Ah, Mrs. Fayne, how nice to see you! It's many weeks since I called, I fear."

"Good-morning, Bishop. You're looking well."

"And how is Madelaine, may I ask? Looking forward to the return of the prodigals, I suppose?"

"Well, yes, Bishop. She *was*. But now we've heard that only Sandra will be home for the holidays. The others have got to stay in London for some show they're doing. So all

Maddy's hopes of opening up the Blue Door Theatre again are smashed."

"Oh, I *am* sorry to hear that. I was looking forward to seeing them all, too. But I expect Maddy is taking it all as philosophically as usual, isn't she?" asked the Bishop.

"Well – er – I'm afraid she isn't, Bishop. We had a little scene at breakfast time, ostensibly over her arithmetic with the result that Maddy has retired to her bedroom and proclaimed a state of siege."

The Bishop tried not to smile.

"Now this is most unfortunate. Most unfortunate. I was just coming up to visit you, but as you are on your way out and Maddy is in a state of siege –"

"Oh, Bishop, I'd be very grateful if you would go up and have a few words with her. She might take some notice. You know that she thinks a great deal of you."

"I will see what I can do, Mrs. Fayne, I promise you. May I have permission to take her out to lunch if she will honour me with her company?"

"Certainly, Bishop. And if you can make her go to school this afternoon it would be a great help."

"But why this sudden aversion to school?" the Bishop wanted to know.

"I expect she's lonely without the other three girls. And she finds the work boring, too, now that her head is so filled with the stage and being an actress."

"Ah, yes, I begin to see light. Well, I will see what I can do. Good-morning, Mrs. Fayne," and he continued up Goldhawk Avenue in the direction of the Faynes' house.

Maddy was just reading aloud a dramatic speech of Mary Queen of Scots before her execution when there was a knock at the front door. "Enter," declaimed Maddy, "I am ready to die –" then she realized it was not merely imaginary noises off, but someone actually at the door.

"Bother!" she thought, "I won't answer, but I'll see who it is." She flung open the window, recoiled at the sight of the familiar gaunt figure of the Bishop, and bumped her head on the window frame. The Bishop looked up.

"Hullo, Maddy. Aren't you going to come down and let me in?"

"No, I can't."

"Why not?"

"I'm locked in my room."

"Oh! And who locked you in?"

"I did."

"Well, can't you unlock yourself?"

"No. I'm in disgrace."

"So I gathered when I met your mother just now. You're having a one-man siege, I suppose? Wouldn't you like to come out and have a breath of fresh air? You could return to your fortress before your mother comes back, if you wished."

"But I told her I was going to stay here until she promised not to tell you about me," Maddy demurred.

"Well, she has told me already, so your stay-in strike seems somewhat useless, doesn't it? Besides, if you continue it you will miss your lunch, whereas if you come down from your tower and accompany me on my morning walk we might finish up by having lunch at Bonner's in the High Street. They have remarkably good duck there on Tuesdays."

Maddy wavered. It was ages since she had seen the Bishop, and there was tons she wanted to say to him. It would be much nicer to be out in the sunshine with the Bishop than to be in disgrace in her bedroom. And lunch at Bonner's –

The Bishop said casually, "One can also have meringues and cream!"

Maddy's mouth watered. "Can you have ice cream with them as well?"

"I shouldn't be at all surprised."

"I'll be down in two ticks, Bishop. Must I wear a hat?"

"No, Maddy. I think mine will furnish enough respectability for two. Hurry up, my dear. I want to get as far as the Fennymead fields if I can, and there's not a great deal of the morning left."

Maddy hurriedly washed the tear-stains from her face and put on her blazer. Soon they were walking down the avenue. Their shadows went before them on the pavement, one tall and stately, the other short and inclined to bounce.

2

THE FENNYMEAD LEGEND

Out in the fields the air was warm and spring-like. Maddy took off her blazer and rolled her stockings down to her ankles. She chased lambs, picked catkins, and got her feet wet in the river, while the Bishop swung along at a steady pace, talking all the time whether Maddy was within hearing distance or not. Maddy was the first to tire.

"Phew! We've walked miles," she gasped, after swinging on the branch of a tree that broke and landed her in a puddle. "Can we sit on this fence, Bishop?" They perched on a stile and surveyed the landscape. "Where are we now, Bishop? I don't think I've been round here very often."

"We're just approaching Fennymead."

"Isn't that where the castle is?"

"Yes." The Bishop pointed with his stick. "You can see some of the turrets among the trees over there."

"Does anyone live there now?" Maddy wanted to know.

"I believe the present Lord Moulcester is still in residence. He's a bit of a hermit, though. They always were a peculiar family."

Maddy dived into her blazer pocket and produced a sticky package.

"Will you have a piece of chocolate, Bishop? It's inclined to be squashy, but it's rather nice."

"Thank you, Maddy, I will." The Bishop took a piece. "Yes, as you say – squashy, but nice. Talking of the castle, by the way, I suppose you know the legend about the Maid of Fennymead?"

Maddy screwed up her face in an effort to appear intelligent.

"Didn't she run away or something because they wanted her to be one of Henry the Eighth's wives?"

The Bishop groaned. "Oh, Maddy, Maddy! Your history is sadly at fault. No, Elizabeth of Fennymead was believed to be a daughter of Catherine of Aragon and Arthur, Prince of Wales. Catherine married him before she married Henry the Eighth, you know. The Maid was kidnapped by a second cousin, Richard, Lord Moulcester, when she was quite young, and held at Fennymead with the intention of placing her forcibly on the throne at the death of Henry the Seventh."

Maddy licked the chocolate wrapping with great care and then said, "Does that mean they were going to make her the queen?"

"That was the idea."

"Then why did she run away?"

"I suppose she didn't want to be queen. She knew that Lord Moulcester would be the ruling power, and she would just be a figure-head."

"And what happened to her?" Maddy wanted to know. "Where did she run to?"

"Nobody knows. Some people say she lost herself in the forest and died, others that she was adopted by a woodcutter and his family. Oh, there are numerous tales as to what happened to the child."

Maddy stared at the Bishop in surprise. "Child? Was she a child? I'd always heard she was grown-up." The Bishop warmed to his subject.

"Oh, yes," he said, "that is the general belief. But in some old manuscripts I found in my library the other day, I discovered some rather interesting verses that throw a little light on the matter. 'Ye Riming Chronicles of Thomas Attewater, sometime Domestic Chaplain to Richard, Earl of Moulcester.' It's all in an illuminated black-letter."

"What's that?" interrupted Maddy.

"Well, black-letter is the mediaeval type of script, and illumination means that the capitals are coloured and have little illustrations inside the letter. I must show you some one day. They are extremely beautifully done."

"And what does it say about this child, Elizabeth?" Maddy wanted to know.

"The whole story is there in rhyming couplets. I can only remember the last two lines – something like this –

> 'At twelve years old away she fledde,
> Forsook her crown but saved her hedde.' "

Maddy repeated it.
"Oh, I like that –

> 'At twelve years old away she fledde,
> Forsook her crown but saved her hedde –'

Why 'saved her head'? Who would have beheaded her?" she wanted to know.

"Henry the Eighth wouldn't have stood for any hanky-panky, I'm afraid," said the Bishop. "The revolt would have been quelled inevitably, and she would have met with the same fate as Perkin Warbeck and Lambert Simnel in the previous reign."

Maddy giggled. "I love Perkin Warbeck and Lambert Simnel. They sound like crosstalk comedians. But what an exciting story – It's just like a film. Not like history at all."

The Bishop said rather disapprovingly, "I believe they are going to film it very soon, as a matter of fact, but I expect they'll make the heroine a 'glamour girl', as they say, with eyelashes yards long, and give her some sort of romantic reason for running away. They'll probably make Robin Hood the hero, or something equally absurd."

"You don't like films, do you, Bishop?"

"In my opinion the good ones are rarely good enough to make up for the bad ones," replied the Bishop.

"I love historical films," enthused Maddy. "They're usually the best. Oh, I wish I lived in history."

"You do, Maddy."

"I don't. I live nowadays."

"But nowadays will prove to be a very important part of history," said the Bishop gravely.

"I mean I'd like to live in times like Elizabeth of Fennymead did," pursued Maddy.

The Bishop saw his chance. "I don't think you would fit in very well," he told her.

"Why not."

"How old are you?" he asked.

"Twelve."

"Well, now, in the days of Elizabeth of Fennymead a girl of twelve was considered well on the way toward being grown up. She wasn't a spoilt baby any more."

Maddy sensed an approaching lecture. "I suppose that's a dig at me, Bishop?"

"Yes, Maddy, it is; because although I have always thought of you as very grown-up and sensible in most ways,

I must admit that I am very disappointed in the childish way you are behaving at the moment. Instead of trying to appear older than you are and working hard so that you can get through school quickly and on to your career, you are merely emphasizing your youth by this stupid refusal to go to school. Think how ashamed the others will be when they hear about it."

Maddy pouted. "They just won't be interested. Why should they? Sandra's written and told me all about what they are doing. They have dancing and fencing and voice production – absolutely everything they've always wanted to learn."

"But don't you see," put the Bishop, "they've had to wait for all the things they've got, just as you are waiting."

"They didn't know they wanted them when they were my age, so it wasn't so bad," retorted Maddy.

"Yes, Maddy, you're right there," agreed the Bishop, "but don't you see that it is you who have the advantage. They have not had so long in which to prepare themselves for their careers. In all this time that you are grumbling so bitterly about, you can be studying different types of people – their accents, their mannerisms, their habits. You can be reading all the great plays there are to be read and all the histories of great actors and actresses of the past, so that when you finally reach Dramatic School you will have a solid foundation of knowledge on which to build your technique."

Maddy sighed heavily. "It's an easy thing to say that, Bishop. But it's not an easy thing to do. How can I meet interesting people in Fenchester? There's no one worth studying; no one with any characteristics at all."

"Now really, Maddy!" exclaimed the Bishop. "How can you say that? What about our friend Mrs. Potter-Smith of the Ladies' Institute? Think what copy you have in her –"

Maddy giggled at the mention of her age-old enemy and then said, "But, Bishop, I don't get a lot of time to read plays and books. I'm always busy with silly old men who *will* dig up fields all time – you know – if A digs half a field quicker than B, why bother about what C does."

The Bishop chuckled. "Well, Maddy, I'm afraid I can't think of anything to add a spice of drama to that, but I do hope that you see the trend of my argument."

Maddy said in a rather small voice that she did.

"And I hope you'll try to make me and your parents and the rest of the Blue Door Company a bit prouder of you in the future."

"All right, Bishop. I promise."

"Good!" The Bishop got off the stile. "I think we had better get back now."

"Just a minute," said Maddy. "I want to have another look at the castle. Doesn't it look lovely from here?" As she looked at the grey towers among the newly green trees she made a mental note to turn over yet another new leaf.

"I think we had better hurry," said the Bishop, "in case all the meringues at Bonner's are gone."

Instantly Maddy bounded from the stile. They kept up a good pace until they were almost in Fenchester again, and then the Bishop said, "Er – Maddy, don't you think that your stockings, perhaps –"

Maddy hastily pulled them up, remarking, "You must be hot in gaiters, Bishop," and they walked sedately down the High Street.

Bonner's smelt as delicious as usual, coffee, and hot cakes and – Maddy sniffed ecstatically – yes, definitely duck. When they were seated at a little table for two, the Bishop noticed that Maddy was still sniffing the air inquiringly.

"What's the matter?" he asked.

"I can smell Californian Poppy," she hissed across the table, in a very audible stage-whisper. "That means Mrs. Potter-Smith."

Sure enough, at the next table sat the leader of the Ladies' Institute, swathed in her moth-eaten furs, and wearing a rather more ridiculous hat than usual.

"Just our luck!" groaned Maddy. It was not long before Mrs. Potter-Smith spotted them.

"Ah, dear Bishop!" she purred. "How nice to see you! And who's this? Oh, why, of course, the little Fayne girl, isn't it? I should have thought you would have been at school today instead of gadding about." Maddy said nothing, but fixed her eyes on the cherries that dangled over Mrs. Potter-Smith's left eye. "Really, Bishop," the oily voice went on, "I'm surprised that you have time for outings like this with all the sick-visiting and other duties that must fall to you."

The Bishop tried to smile.

"Well, I'm just leaving now. I'm afraid you'll find most things off the menu by this time. Oh, one moment, Maddy dear, your pigtail is undone – So hard to keep children tidy, isn't it?" She gave Maddy's pigtail a vigorous pull as she retied it. "Well – bai-bai," and she waddled off on stilt-like heels.

Maddy heaved a sigh. "Thank goodness she's gone before the duck arrives or I should have lost my appetite. What an old hag."

"Mrs. Potter-Smith is the mainstay of the Ladies' Institute, a benefactress to many good causes, and an indefatigable church worker," the Bishop reproved her.

"And yet you still think the same of her as I do," added Maddy. "Funny, isn't it?"

The duck and green peas, followed by meringue and cream with ice-cream as well, was delicious. When they had finished and were sipping coffee out of what Maddy called "teddy bears' cups" the Bishop said casually, "I'm walking up towards your school, so I may as well come with you."

Sitting at her desk that afternoon Maddy reflected that at least she had missed arithmetic.

MADDY FINDS A FRIEND

As the train steamed in, Maddy, standing on the platform, could not help feeling a little bit excited. Although only Sandra was returning, at least she would hear all about Dramatic School and the adventures of the term. Sandra stepped off the train looking smart in a new suit. Maddy noticed that she didn't look very good-tempered.

"Oh, hullo! I wondered whether you'd come to meet me," Sandra said when Maddy bounced up to her. "Stay here a minute. I've got to get some luggage out of the van." And she disappeared. All the welcoming words that Maddy had prepared were wasted. When Sandra reappeared she was worried over a case that had gone astray and scarcely seemed to notice Maddy.

"We'll get a taxi," said Sandra at the station exit.

"Whatever for?" asked Maddy. "We can easily walk." But Sandra had hailed a taxi and Maddy was really quite pleased as she could wave to her little school friends as they went through the town. At last Maddy sat back and said, "I'm awfully glad you've come home."

Sandra said wryly, "I wish I could say the same. I was livid when I found that my part of the show was cut."

"What a shame!" said Maddy, then, timidly, "We could do a little show on our own, perhaps –"

"Don't be silly," said Sandra. "How could we, without the others?" Then she lapsed into silence.

Maddy realized once more that the days of the Blue Door Theatre shows were over, and that a great gulf separated her from the others – the gulf of Not Being at Dramatic School.

During the days that followed Maddy saw very little of Sandra, who was either out shopping with her mother or writing long letters to friends at Dramatic School of whom Maddy had never heard. Maddy was struggling with end-of-term exams, and as she had left all her revision until too late, she was beginning to regret it.

One Saturday morning she was doing some equations with the help of her mother and Sandra when suddenly everything became too much for her. Just as they had worked out three different answers to the same question the sun burst out from behind some clouds and shone on to Maddy's trusty bicycle which stood outside the window. She jumped up, spilling the ink.

"Where are you off to?" cried her mother.

"Out," shouted Maddy, leaping on to her bicycle. She rattled down the avenue, instinctively making for the road to Browcliffe, the nearest seaside town. It did not take her very long to get there, for she rode as if demented, trying to escape from the chains of equations that seemed to bind her.

At Browcliffe the sun seemed brighter, the tide was in, and the fun fair on the pier was in full swing. She parked her bicycle, reflecting that no one ever seemed to want to steal it, and walked along the pier. Occasionally she stopped and bent down to peer through the cracks in the boards at the churning green sea below. A mixture of exciting noises came from the fun fair; the music of the merry-go-rounds, the screams of people on the switchback, and the crashes of the little brightly painted bumper cars. She watched the switchback and the bumper cars for a long time before she could decide on which to spend her only three pence. The switchback was exciting, but the bumper cars lasted longer. Then she discovered that the switchback was sixpence anyhow, so that decided it. She paid her three pence and stepped into the little scarlet racing car. There was only one other person on the course, a rather lanky youth with spectacles. But it was his clothes that made Maddy stare. He wore a brilliant lumber jacket of red and green check, green corduroy trousers, suede shoes, and a red spotted scarf round his neck. Maddy cruised round quite contentedly for a while and then began to want excitement. It wasn't much fun when there was no one to bump into. The boy in the blue car was dawdling along in front of her. The temptation was too great. She trod on the accelerator and held on for dear life. There was a terrific crash and the boy was shot several inches into the air. "You little horror," he shouted. "You've broken my back. Just you wait till I catch up with you."

Maddy laughed delightedly and dodged away crying, "You can't catch me – you can't catch me –"

"Can't I just!" There followed an exciting chase round and round the arena.

"Take that!" He crashed into her from sideways on.

"You roadhog!" yelled Maddy.

"Roadhog! Why, you're a public enemy. I'm coming after you –" but with a grinding sound the machinery began to slow down.

"Oh, they're stopping the cars!" said Maddy, disappointed.

"Perhaps it's just as well" said the boy as he got out. "Phew – you've shaken me to bits. How about something to drink at that stall over there?"

"Rather," agreed Maddy. "Only I'm broke."

"Doesn't matter. I'm not." They made their way through the maze of side shows and shooting galleries to a refreshment booth loaded with sticky buns and drinks of varying hues.

"What's it going to be?" asked her new friend. "The lemonade looks a bit vivid."

"I like it vivid," said Maddy. "It tastes better."

"O.K." He ordered two lemonades from the buxom lady behind the counter, who eyed his clothes with interest.

"May I have two straws?" asked Maddy. "You can drink it quicker that way." Her glass was soon nearly empty, and she was making bubbly noises through her straws. "M-m – That was lovely!" she sighed. "And it might be even better if we had one of those squidgy buns." The boy laughed.

"You have one. I won't. I have my digestion to think of."

"I don't think about mine much," Maddy told him. "Except when I'm really hungry."

"Aren't you 'really hungry' now?" the boy asked with interest.

"Oh, no," said Maddy. "This is only being peckish."

"What a constitution!"

"I tell you what," suggested Maddy, eyeing the fairground again. "We could go on the switchback –"

The boy groaned. "Lurid lemonade, squidgy buns, and then you talk of switchbacks!"

Maddy was surprised. "Why? Don't you think it's a good idea?"

"The idea's all right – but I doubt if I dare put it into practice. Besides, I'm afraid I'll have to be going soon. The sun's come out, so I shall have to work this afternoon."

This was puzzling to Maddy. "What on earth has the sun to do with it?"

"I'm working on the film at Fenchester," said the boy, draining his lemonade.

"What film?" asked Maddy, goggle-eyed.

"The Fennymead film. We're on location down by the castle."

"On location?"

"Yes, you know – shooting out of doors – all that sort of thing."

Maddy looked at him with renewed interest. "But you're not an actor, are you?"

"Why don't you think I am?"

"Well, actors usually look even more conceited than you do," she told him frankly. He laughed.

"You're right. I'm not an actor. I'm a musician. A composer, in fact. I'm supposed to be composing the music for the film, and so I'm here to watch the shooting and hope for inspiration."

"You're not old enough to be a composer," said Maddy disbelievingly.

"I'm nineteen," he retorted. "That's quite old enough."

"What other films have you composed for?" Maddy wanted to know.

"Well – er – this is my first, but I've done lots of other kinds of musical work." He zipped his lumber jacket up to the neck and said carelessly, "In fact my name is Rodney Randall."

"Oh! Mine's Maddy." Rodney looked rather hurt.

"Haven't you ever heard my name before?"

"No."

"Oh, perhaps you'd have been too young at the time," he said in a somewhat patronizing tone. "Ever heard of the River Symphony? I wrote it when I was fifteen. I was a child prodigy." But Maddy was unimpressed.

"Yes. I'm one too. It's horrid isn't it?"

"You're one?" he exclaimed. "What on earth do you do?"

"I act," announced Maddy, helping herself to another squidgy bun, and leaving Rodney to pay for it.

"Really? What have you been in?"

Maddy said airily, "Oh, this and that, you know. On and off. Whenever I get the chance."

"Yes, opportunity is a fine thing," Rodney agreed bitterly. "What they expect me to compose *on* down here I can't imagine. There's a piano in my digs, but as soon as I start to play the landlady puts her head round the door and says, 'Now, ain't that luverly, sir, ain't that just luverly –' Oh, for my baby grand at home!"

"Where's home?"

"London."

"Everyone seems to live in London except me," said Maddy discontentedly, feeding a seagull with the remains of her squidgy bun.

"Oh, London's all right," said Rodney. "But it's nice to get into the country for a change. I should love it down here if only I had a decent piano."

"Well, what about me?" said Maddy. "I've only got a mouth organ." She reflected for a minute and then said, "I tell you what, though – I could lend you the piano in – in my theatre –"

"Your theatre?"

"Yes. It's not a particularly good piano, but at least you wouldn't have anyone telling you it was luverly."

"That's terrific!" exclaimed Rodney. "Where is your theatre?"

"In Fenchester," Maddy told him. "It's called the Blue Door Theatre. You see, the door is blue. I'll show you. How did you come? By bike?"

Rodney nodded. "Good. So did I. Let's hurry back and I'll take you round before lunch."

They found their bicycles and raced back, doing "flying angels" down all the hills. When they got into Fenchester Maddy led him through many by-ways and short cuts of her own invention to Pleasant Street, where the little Blue Door Theatre was squashed in between some warehouses. Maddy reflected that it looked very different from their first sight of it, nearly four years previously, for they had kept it smartly painted and the blue and brown sign still hung over the door.

"What an intriguing little place!" exclaimed Rodney.

Maddy felt under a brick and found the key. The door was opened and she switched on the lights showing the neat little hall with chairs arranged in rows, and the blue curtains hiding the stage. Rodney immediately pounced on the piano and made the rafters ring with something that he said was Rimsky-Korsakoff. Maddy danced madly round the theatre and finally flung herself down on the floor.

"I like that Rimsky-Whatnot bloke," she said. "Play some more."

Rodney played for a while longer and then said, "You know, Maddy, you're a very lucky child, having a theatre like this."

"H'm! Lucky!" growled Maddy. "I'm not really. I'm embittered, that's what I am! I'm an embittered woman!"

"Nonsense, Maddy. What on earth have you got to be embittered about?"

Maddy poured out all her troubles about the other members of the Blue Door Theatre Company staying in London for the holidays, and Sandra's disappointing behaviour.

"Cheer up!" said Rodney, thumping her on the back. "You and I can give a recital together – me on the piano and you on your mouth organ."

"Oh, Rodney, don't tease me when I'm so unhappy. There's simply nothing to look forward to."

"Well, if you want some excitement," suggested Rodney, "how about coming down with me to see the filming some time?"

"What was that, Rodney?" breathed Maddy. "Say that again –"

Rodney repeated his invitation. "I said, 'Will you come down on to the location with me sometime?'"

"Will I? Will I?" squealed Maddy. "Boy, oh boy! I thought I'd have to work up to it for weeks before I'd get you to say that." Maddy executed a violent tap dance on the wooden stage, although Rodney was trying to play Handel. Then she noticed the time. As usual she was horribly and irrevocably late for lunch.

"Bye-bye, Rodney. See you here tomorrow morning!" and she leaped on her bike and pedalled madly for home, losing a hair ribbon as she turned a corner.

4

MADDY IN FILMLAND

Maddy sat on the fence anxiously watching the end of the road. Rodney had promised to take her down to the location, "the lot," as he called it, and he was a quarter of an hour late. At last a flash of colour on a bicycle appeared and Maddy leaped on to hers and rode to meet him.

"Hiya," she said. "Thought you were never coming."

"Sorry. We'd better hurry, they're going to shoot today."

"Well, what on earth have they been doing all this time?" Maddy wanted to know.

"Oh, getting sets up, collecting extras, and generally wasting time."

The Fennymead fields were teeming with activity. The film company had erected a whole encampment of little huts and tents. There were hundreds of people walking about in gaily coloured, sixteenth-century costumes and brilliant make-up, mixed with technicians and mechanics in shirt sleeves and dungarees. The scene that was being shot appeared to be the village green with a maypole on it, and little imitation houses had been built round three sides of one of the fields.

"Oh, isn't it lovely!" gasped Maddy. "They look just like real little houses."

On a hillock overlooking the set was a very fat man wearing a red beret, sun glasses, and a megaphone through which he kept up a continual stream of command to the people around him in broken English which was double-Dutch to Maddy. There was also a microphone so that people down on the set could hear when he spoke to them.

"That's Van Velden," said Rodney, lowering his voice reverently.

"Who's he?" asked Maddy.

"Haven't you ever heard of him? He makes all the best English films."

"But he's not English," objected Maddy.

"No, he's Dutch. And oh boy, what a director!"

"Who are all the little men sitting round him?" Maddy wanted to know.

"They're his assistant directors and script writers, and what he calls his 'authenticity men'."

"What are they?"

"People who know all about the correct historical details of what he's filming. He's a stickler for authenticity."

"Who's the young man with side whiskers and a pipe?"

"That's Dent, the chief assistant director. He does all the dirty work. He's a good sort, though."

Just then Dent bellowed through the mike, "On your marks, please. We're going to shoot." Instantly the scene on the village green began to take shape. Girls grouped themselves round the maypole, a little village band squatted on a bank and miscellaneous villagers took up their positions.

"Take off those coats, please!" roared Dent. Some of the crowd who had their own coats slung round their shoulders hastily pushed them behind pieces of scenery.

"Will someone call Miss Warren, please?" From a little hut on the outskirts came a slender dark-haired figure in a green frock, accompanied by her dresser, who carried her coat and a little canvas chair with her name on it.

"That's Felicity Warren," said Rodney. "Isn't she lovely?"

"Felicity Warren," repeated Maddy. "Is she a well-known actress?"

"Yes, but only on the stage. This is her first film."

Maddy remembered all of a sudden. "Of course! I saw her play Juliet at Stratford-on-Avon, when the Bishop took us there. She's awfully clever."

"I'll introduce you to her if we get a chance," said Rodney.

Maddy bounced on the green turf delightedly. "Oh, how lovely! This is the most exciting day of my life! Oh, look. What's happening now?"

"They're going to shoot a scene in a minute. But there seems to be something wrong with the cameras now." Rodney looked anxiously at the sky. "And if they're not careful the sun will have gone in."

"I can't see awfully well, Rodney. Can't we go over on the slope up there?"

"O.K. But don't disturb the old man." They walked over and stood just behind the director's chair.

"He's not old," objected Maddy, taking a closer look at the round face below the beret. "He's quite young. It's only that he's tubby. Why does he wear a beret?"

Van Velden swung round. "Madame. I vear a beret becos mitout a beret mine head is cold. Who is zis leetle girl, Rodney? Your seester? Your fiancée?"

"No, Mr. Van Velden. This is a little friend of mine called Maddy. This is Mr. Van Velden."

Maddy held out her hand and he grasped it in such a grip that she nearly squealed. "Hullo," Maddy said. "I've never met a Dutchman before. I've never met a film director before. In fact I've never been on a film set before." Van Velden beamed.

"You like it, eh? Well, Rodney, watch zat she sees all she wishes. Now I must to my vork get back." He boomed through the mike, "Everybodies on ze set, plis. Everybodies on ze set. Miss Varren, would you come a minute, plis."

"Here she comes," whispered Maddy. "What part is she playing?"

"Elizabeth of Fennymead, of course."

Maddy goggled.

"But she can't be – she was only a little girl." Rodney looked at her as if she were half-witted.

"Don't be silly. She elopes. Look, Russell Durrant is playing the woodcutter she elopes with."

"Nonsense," said Maddy firmly –

> " 'At twelve years old away she fledde,
> Forsook her crown, but saved her hedde.' "

Rodney was puzzled. "What on earth? I don't get it."

Maddy repeated the couplet, adding, "The Bishop told me that he found it in some old book. It was a rhyming something-or-other of Thomas Someone, a chaplain to the Earl of Moulcester at the time that Elizabeth escaped."

Rodney whistled. "You're *sure* about that?"

"Perfectly."

Van Velden had finished talking to Felicity Warren and now she returned to the set and the cameras were ready.

"O.K. Silence, plis. We are ready to go. On your marks. O.K. cameras?"

"O.K." came the reply from the little men buzzing around the two massive cameras.

"O.K. for sound?"

"O.K." A little boy holding large wooden clappers stepped in front of the camera. Attached to the clappers was a blackboard on which was chalked "Forsaken Crown, Scene 5, Take 1." He held this up to the camera which had started to make a whirring sound, and repeated it in a piping little voice.

"Action!" roared Van Velden.

Instantly the scene came alive, as if a penny had been put in a slot to make the dolls dance. The fiddlers played an old folk tune, the girls circled round the maypole, and the villagers danced as well. The camera "tracked", pushed slowly forward on a trolley, up to Felicity Warren dancing with a tall man wearing leather jerkin and hose. This was evidently Russell Durrant.

"Cut!" yelled Van Velden. "It is no good."

Rodney said to Maddy, "Do you think Van Velden knows that jingle? I'm sure he doesn't. I'd never heard it before."

"Nor had I until the other day," said Maddy. "I don't think it's been known at all until now. The Bishop is writing up to the Antiquary – the Anti – oh, you know, that society –"

Rodney seemed stunned. "Goodness! What will Van Velden say? I think we ought to tell him."

Once more all the preliminaries were gone through and Van Velden yelled "Action!" This time it seemed more to his liking, but in the middle the sun went in.

"Cut!" roared Van Velden. "Break for five minutes!" At once all the dancing dolls flopped on to the grass and produced either sandwiches or newspapers and gossiped amongst themselves. Felicity Warren's chair was brought for her, and Russell Durrant had a drink from a thermos flask.

"Don't they waste a lot of time?" said Maddy. "Not like real acting at all." But Rodney was still worrying over the information that Maddy had come out with. The clapper boy shouted "Scene 5, Take 6," before sound, sun, and actors had all combined to satisfy Van Velden.

"Cut!" he yelled. "Zat is very O.K. You are goot children! Go drink some tea." The lot cleared like magic. Rodney saw his chance. "Excuse me, sir –" But Van Velden was poring over the script with the continuity girl.

"Not now, Rodney, plis. I am concentrationing."

"But please, sir –"

"Quiet, plis," he roared. "I cannot listen to myself thinking."

"But if you'd just let me –"

"Not now, boy!" shouted Van Velden, pushing his beret to the back of his head and wiping his brow with an enormous handkerchief. "Some talk with Miss Warren I now must haf."

Dent shouted through the mike, "Miss Warren, please."

Felicity walked over to them.

"Oh dear, whatever shall we do!" whispered Maddy.

"I don't know whether we should tell him or not," said Rodney.

Van Velden was talking to Felicity, who listened attentively. "This take ve now vill make, Felicity. Your lines you know? Goot! Ver' tender and sincere it must be. Look straight at ze woodcutter's face and he vill look at you ver' lovinkly – you see?"

"Does he know she's only twelve years old?" asked Maddy in stentorian tones. Van Velden wrung his hands.

"Quiet, plis. I vish to make concentrationing."

But Felicity had heard. She turned and looked at Maddy. "What did that child say?"

"Nozzing. Nozzing." Van Velden waved his arms. "She is Rodney's mother – no, his sister – no, I mistake me –"

"You certainly do mistake you if you're having Miss Warren to play Elizabeth of Fennymead," said Maddy bluntly. "Don't you know she was only twelve?"

"What?" exclaimed Felicity. Maddy recited,

> " 'At twelve years old away she fledde,
> Forsook her crown, but saved her hedde.' "

"Quiet, plis. For nursery rhymes I haf no time. Now, Miss Warren –"

But Felicity was holding Maddy by the shoulders and almost shaking her. "Where did you hear that?" she asked tensely.

"It's an old rhyme that's just been discovered."

"Meaning – Elizabeth of Fennymead?" asked Felicity, in horror.

"Yes," said Rodney. "The Bishop of Fenchester has just discovered some manuscripts of the time that prove that she was only twelve when she ran away."

"Good heavens!" cried Felicity. "Hans! Did you hear that?"

Van Velden was writhing in his chair with impatience so that Maddy feared he might come through the canvas. "Vot is all this? Vill someone to me explain! Plis, thank you, yes!"

Felicity had gone pale. "Denny!" she called to the chief assistant. "Do come here! I can't believe it! After all this – My first film – Oh, Rodney, are you sure it's true?"

"Well, Maddy says the Bishop told her."

"I can't believe it!" breathed Felicity.

"Vot is this? Vot is this?" roared Van Velden.

Dent had joined the group and was wanting to know the trouble. "Listen, Hans. This little girl is a friend of the Bishop of Fenchester. He has discovered papers that prove that Elizabeth was only a little girl. What's the rhyme, Rodney?"

They chorused it in unison. Van Velden repeated it under his breath. For a long time he was silent and then a mighty roar shook him.

"Vot are my authenticity men doing? I demand of you – I demand of them – Mr. Dingle – Mr. Hassock – Where from did you get your facts? My time and my money you haf wasted. You haf ze sack. Gootbye."

Two rather pathetic little men got up and slunk away. Maddy felt very sorry for them. It was all her fault.

"Never mind!" Rodney whispered to her. "He'll take them back in the end. He always does."

Van Velden now crumpled up in his chair. "And a headache now I haf – Vill someone an aspirin plis provide. So, Miss Warren. You vill play Elizabeth as twelve years old – "

Felicity said bitterly but firmly, "Oh no I will not. If I've got to play mutton dressed up as lamb I'll go back to the stage to do it."

Van Velden moaned piteously, "But twelve years old you could look if ve vork hard on you – if my make-up men are not half-vitted too."

Felicity stamped her foot. "No. No. No. And that's final. You'll have to cancel my contract."

"But Felicity," pleaded Dent, "don't you think you could –"

There was complete chaos for several minutes while he tried to persuade Felicity to be more reasonable. Maddy apologized to anyone who would listen, and Van Velden raged and screamed like a wild thing. Several of the extras drifted up, and hearing the excitement called their friends. Soon the whole set was gathered round listening eagerly.

"Perhaps the public won't mind," said Rodney. "Only a few people know –"

"I'm not playing Elizabeth!" cried Felicity. "Either correctly as twelve or incorrectly at any age. I'm going back to the stage as quickly as I can. I'm sick of this whole racket."

"But your contract –" roared Van Velden. "I have you under contract. If you break it I will persecute you." His sun glasses were pushed up on to his forehead, and at intervals he jumped on his red beret.

Dent tried to pacify everyone. "Look. The sun has come out. Let's get on."

"Get on! Get on!" shouted Van Velden. "Vot is there to get on vith? I am ruined – finished – all through this awful child. Oh, vot a wretch am I! Surrounded so by dolt heads. Someone plis an aspirin gif –" He collapsed once more into his chair which sagged ominously. "And coffee, plis. Strong and black."

"I think I'd better go home," said Maddy in a small voice. As she left the location behind her a babble of voices still floated to her on the wind.

5

THE FILM TEST

Denny Dent knocked cautiously at the door of the hut that served Van Velden for an office. For a whole week the director had been cloistered here puzzling over the problem of what to do about the film. Rumours had spread that the whole project was to be dropped, that Felicity would play Elizabeth as twelve, that Felicity would play Elizabeth as twenty, that Felicity would not play Elizabeth at all. The last was true. Once Felicity had put her foot down there was no moving her.

"I will play any other part in the film you choose to give me," she had announced, "but not Elizabeth – at any age."

"Then you shall play Margaret, the maid," said Van Velden, expecting more fireworks at this suggestion that the star should play a minor role.

"Very well," said Felicity calmly. "I should prefer that. But only on one condition – that a child is found to play Elizabeth and the script is rewritten."

And so it was settled. Dent had been instructed to wire to London for photos and particulars of any children that the company had under contract, and any that the dramatic schools and academies could suggest. Dent held another large packet of photos which had just arrived. He knocked again and received a muffled "Come" from Van Velden. He went in. The desk was covered with empty coffee cups, aspirin bottles, and photos of young film stars.

"Vot is it?" snapped Van Velden.

"Some more photos, sir."

"Ach! I am sick of these simpering faces. Of not one could I make a star. These are not real children. They do not inspire me. They do not fit for ze character my script-writers are creating."

Dent looked at some of them. "They're certainly not particularly photogenic. What about this little dark one?"

"Too thin –"

"Or this kid we had in the Somerset Maugham thing –"

"Too fat."

Dent picked out another. "What about her?"

"Too old."

"Or this one?"

"Too young. It is no good. None of these haf anythink. I vill go out into the streets and fine ten better. We want someone who is –" Van Velden waved his hands in an effort to express himself.

"Now, look here, sir," said Dent. "What sort of girl *do* you want? If we make up our minds exactly, it might be easier. Fair or dark? How old? How tall?"

Van Velden shut his eyes as if in a trance. "Oh, Denny, I 'ave thought till I am blue of the face. She should look twelve, about five foots her height should be, ver' blonde as Felicity is dark and so is Russell, but above all, she must haf no curls, no dimples – only a face that vill interest young and old, *and*, zis we seem to forget, an ability to act she must haf."

"Such as whom?" asked Denny, filling his pipe.

Van Velden frowned and took another aspirin. "I do not know. A picture I haf in my mind, but where from it came I cannot tell. It is a child I haf seen lately since we haf left town –"

"One of the extras perhaps," Denny suggested.

"Perhaps. It was here on ze lot –"

Denny laughed. "You don't mean that awful child who's caused all the trouble?"

Van Velden leaped from his chair. "But yes! Rodney's sister! The very one. Zat is the face I haf been seeing all zis time."

"But – she's such a funny little thing –"

"Yes, yes. But did you notice what animation – and ze structure of her face is original."

"But can she act?" demurred Denny.

"About that ve vill see. Now, will you fetch Rodney and tell him to find at once zis little girl."

"We could give her a test, I suppose," agreed Dent unwillingly, "but hadn't I better get some of the other kids down as well?"

"No," said Van Velden firmly. "First ve try zis child. I am not a superstitious man, but if she was sent to us causing all zis trouble, zen perhaps vith a purpose she was sent."

Dent sighed heavily and went in search of Rodney, whom he found lying asleep under the maypole, his head on a pile of music manuscript.

"You look as if you're working hard," said the assistant director, digging him in the middle with his foot.

Rodney woke up and yawned. "What's cooking, Denny?" he wanted to know.

"You know that kid who brought up all this business about Elizabeth only being twelve," began Denny.

"Yes. But you can't blame her. It was a jolly good job she did point out the mistake."

"Quite," agreed Denny. "What I want to know is, can she act?"

"Yes," said Rodney. "How did you know?"

"Know what?"

"That she acts."

"I didn't. Does she?"

"Yes. She's crazy about it."

"Well then, go and see Van Velden. He's crazy too, and wants you to get her for a test."

Rodney leaped up. "Boy, oh Boy! There'll be no holding her. Thanks a lot." And he streaked off in the direction of Van Velden's hut.

It was not long before Rodney was banging on the door of the Faynes' house. Maddy opened it.

"Hullo, Rodney! What's the news?"

"Here is the news," replied Rodney ecstatically, "and this is Rodney Randall simply gloating over it. Miss Madelaine Fayne is asked to report on location at ten o'clock tomorrow morning."

"What for?" asked Maddy. "They can't blame me."

"They're not going to blame you, my child. They're going to test you. They're going to see how you film, because they want you to play Elizabeth of Fennymead."

"Don't be silly, Rodney. Don't tease me."

Rodney produced an envelope. "Well, if you don't believe me – Here's a note from Van Velden."

Maddy said in a shaky voice, "You read it. I couldn't."

Rodney read, "Dear Miss Fayne, – Come please, tomorrow of the morning ten o'clock and we will shoot you. Hans Van Velden."

Maddy laughed rather hysterically. "Oh, how funny! I'm going to be shot! Oh gosh! I never did!" Suddenly she was scared. "But Rodney, what shall I wear? What shall I have to do?"

"It'll be quite easy," Rodney told her. "They'll just give you a little bit to act in front of the camera, and I should think that as long as you act naturally, you should be all right. Perhaps you might throw in a little more grace than usual as it's a costume film. They might even let you wear a costume, which would help."

Realization dawned on Maddy. "Gosh! Gosh! Gosh!" she cried. "Excuse me a minute." She ran into the house crying, "Mummy! Mummy! I'm going to be a film star."

The make-up room smelt delicious – a sort of super-greasepaint smell. Maddy was so excited she could hardly sit still in the chair, and the little make-up man had great difficulty in wrapping a white robe round her and tying her hair back in a white turban. Maddy looked at the array of pastes and paints on the dressing-table.

"Are you going to put all that stuff on me?" she asked.

"Yes," said the make-up man. "It's a very special sort as this is in technicolour."

"Oo-er!" said Maddy. "Shall I come out all different colours?"

"Yes. Pretty as a picture." He set to work on her just as if he were painting a picture, first working in the yellowy foundation, then using brushes to elongate her eyebrows and eyes and to shape her lips. After a final powdering Maddy could scarcely believe her eyes. As he took off her turban she clasped her pig-tails anxiously. "You're not going to cut these off, are you?" she asked.

"No, don't worry." The make-up man brushed and combed her hair with expert fingers and left it hanging loose. "Now

I'll take you along to the wardrobe and see if we can find something to fit you." The wardrobe was packed with six-teenth-century costumes of every description, but it took a long time to find something to fit Maddy. At last a very simple dress of blue velvet was found, and she slipped it on. Looking at her reflection in the mirror she wished that the rest of the Blue Doors could see her. But perhaps one day they would – on the screen.

"I *must* be good enough," she thought, and racked her brains for all that Lynette had ever told her about acting. When she was all ready one of the assistant directors, a cheerful-looking young woman in slacks called Peggy, took her out on to the set. It was a lovely sunny day, and some of the technicians were playing cricket in a corner. There was no sign as yet of Van Velden.

Dent came hurrying up with some sheets of type-written paper. "Hullo, there!" he said, "you look very glamorous. Doesn't she, Peggy? Here's your script. Look it over for a bit. It's not very long. It's when she's first taken to the castle by the wicked uncle. Here, sit down on this chair. I don't suppose Van Velden will be out yet."

Maddy sat down and studied her script. Dent, Peggy, and Rodney drifted off and reappeared with the inevitable cups of tea that seemed to be consumed at all hours. Suddenly Maddy began to be scared. Suppose she failed now. Her parents would think she was no good at all and would not allow her to go to Dramatic School. The rest of the Blue Door Company would feel that she had let them down. In fact, the whole of her future career seemed to rest on how she appeared through the eyes of that horrid great camera over there. There was a light touch on her shoulder and she looked up. It was Felicity Warren, who said "Hullo. You're Madelaine, aren't you? I'm afraid we were hardly introduced properly the other day, were we?"

"Hullo," said Maddy. "I expect you're furious with me, aren't you? I'm sorry. I didn't mean to try and take your part away from you or anything."

Felicity laughed. "Of course you didn't. I'm very glad that you did enlighten us. It would have been awful if we'd made the film and discovered the mistake afterwards. And I'm going to play quite a nice part. I'm going to play Margaret, your maid."

"How do you know I'll be accepted to play Elizabeth?" said Maddy gloomily.

"I'm pretty sure you will be," Felicity told her reassuringly. "You're just the type Van Velden wants."

"But I haven't got the slightest idea how to act for films," began Maddy.

"Well, I'm not particularly qualified to give advice on the subject, but as compared with the stage, I advise you to under-act if anything, and not to speak as loud as you do on the stage, even though you are out-of-doors. Don't look at the camera and don't look down. That's all I can think of. Here comes Van Velden. Good luck, Maddy."

"Goot-morning." Van Velden lumbered up. "So here we haf Rodney's sister –"

"I'm *not* Rodney's sister. I'm Madelaine Fayne," said Maddy firmly. "But you can call me Maddy."

"Thank you, Madame!" Van Velden bowed from what would have been his waist if he had had one. Then he looked hard at her from every angle, walking round her several times and saying, "H'm!" thoughtfully. Dent and Peggy came and joined him and they all walked round her and said, "H'm!" till Maddy felt quite embarrassed.

"O.K.," said Van Velden. "Now ve vill shoot. Cameras, plis! Miss Fayne, will you plis stand over there by the maypole and first just do as I tell you." When the camera was whirring

he said, "Now walk plis towards me and smile ver' happily."
Maddy didn't feel like smiling, in fact her knees were knock-
ing. Rodney, standing behind Van Velden, saw this and made
an extremely funny face at her that almost made her laugh
outright. She walked happily up towards the camera until she
almost banged into it.

"Cut!" said Van Velden. "Ver goot. Now stand just here,
and could you plis look ver' sad and perhaps cry just a leetle."

This was easy for Maddy for it was one of the things at
which she had excelled in the Blue Door Theatre shows.
Instantly she burst into such floods of tears with such alacrity
that she made all the onlookers laugh with surprise. She soon
ceased, saying, "That's enough, or I shan't be able to stop."

These exercises seemed to break the ice and the piece which
she had learned from the script seemed quite fun. A rustic
bridge was brought in front of the camera and she had to stand
on it and address her uncle, who was out of camera range.

"Zis I want rather childish and frightened, realizing ze possibilities of danger that lie ahead. Your uncle, he has brought
you on a long journey and now you see for ze first time zis
castle, not looking as now, all beautiful and sunshine, but as
in a thunderstorm. You understand me?"

"Yes, yes, I know how," cried Maddy, running to the bridge
and eager to begin.

"Just a minute," said Van Velden. "Speak plis to test ze
sound."

"Hullo, Mr. Sound-Man. Can you hear me?" said Maddy
in the direction of the mike that hung above her head.

"O.K. for sound," came the reply.

"Action!" shouted Van Velden.

Maddy clutched the side of the bridge, her gaze fixed on
Denny Dent who was "standing in" for her uncle. In her imagi-

nation she added a black beard and heavy eyebrows to the assistant director's pleasant face and wrapped him in a black cloak. Her lines came easily. "Where are you taking me to? What is this place? I don't like it. You must take me home at once!" Denny read Lord Moulcester's lines quite well and at the end, instead of just tailing off as the script did, Maddy turned and ran back across the bridge picking up her skirts in fright.

"Cut!" shouted Van Velden. "Thank you, leetle one. Now you may wash your face and go home."

Maddy felt herself near to tears. "You mean – I'm no good?"

"No, no, my dear! But first, before we do any decisioning these rushes we must see."

Maddy immediately thought of Moses at the word "rushes", but Rodney hastily explained that he only meant they must see projected the little piece of film that she had just made. In spite of the fact that Rodney, Peggy, and Dent, and Felicity all congratulated her, Maddy went home very down-hearted at not knowing the verdict immediately.

The next three days were unbearable for Maddy and also for Sandra and her mother, who assured Maddy that she was "impossible to live with". On the third day when Maddy ran to the door the postman handed her a long buff envelope. Stamped in the corner in red letters were the words, "Urgent. Contract for Signature."

The postman was very upset when Maddy embraced him and burst into tears on his shoulder.

6

MADDY, FILM STAR

There was a paragraph about it in the Fenchester paper, "Local Girl in Fennymead Film". Sandra rang up the rest of the Blue Doors in London, "My dears! What *do* you think?" And Mrs. Potter-Smith simply effervesced at the Ladies' Institute to her bosom friend, Miss Thropple.

"But have you heard the latest – about that little girl Madelaine Fayne? Well, of course we know that those children were always doing odd things, and their parents ought to know better, but this really is a little near the mark. I mean, amateur theatricals – yes, but to let a young child mix with those dissolute film people – well, you should just see the clothes they wear –" She shook her head and clucked her teeth and Miss Thropple joined with a "Well-I-never" expression. "Just frittering the child's time away when she ought to be at school."

Although the school holidays would be over long before the film was finished, it was arranged that on the days she was filming, Maddy should have a governess down on the set to give her the five-hours-a-day tuition insisted upon by the law.

"But we can't afford a governess!" Mrs. Fayne had cried when Van Velden interviewed her on this matter.

"Do not worry yourself, Madame! This is on ze studios!" All sorts of things seemed to be "on the studios". Maddy found that she was to have a car to take her to and from the location.

"How silly!" she said. "I can easily bike."

"But zis is so you may always be early. You understand?"

"Oh, I see," said Maddy. "I thought there was a catch in it."

And then there was something called "Publicity". One day some funny men with little notebooks and cameras turned up on the lot and she had to pose for "stills" which she hated. Moving about and acting in front of cameras was fun, but being stuck in stupid positions, grinning up at Russell Durrant, or sitting in the canteen drinking milk, which she hated, annoyed her intensely.

"And how does it feel to be famous?" asked one of these men, who never seemed to take his hat off.

"I don't know," said Maddy. "How does it?" The man recorded this in his notebook delightedly.

"But don't you realize," he told her, "that you are the most envied child star of the day?"

"Hey, hold on!" said Maddy. "I haven't made the film yet, so I can't be a star." But she was certainly treated as one and sometimes it was a nuisance. While eating her beautifully pre-pared meal in the artistes' canteen with Miss Garrard, the governess, trying to make her consume the right sort of vita-mins, she often eyed with envy the children among the extras who sat on the grass outside munching sandwiches and drink-ing fizzy lemonade out of bottles. But it was certainly nice to have her own dressing-room. It was really a suite of little rooms. From outside the hut did not look very imposing except for "Miss Madelaine Fayne" painted on the door. Inside, it was decorated with pink curtains, an immense long mirror, a dress-ing table, and wardrobe. Next door was a little sitting-room furnished with two desks where she did her lessons, and next door to that a bathroom with a shower, under which Maddy splashed happily for as long as Miss Garrard would allow her.

Poor Miss Garrard had a very hard time of it. She was devoted to Maddy and would call her "sweetie", which made Maddy feel she wanted to kick her. Many times a day Maddy hurt Miss Garrard's tender feelings and left her near to tears in the dressing-room. On returning she would mumble an embarrassed apology which would only increase the bombardment of "sweetie" and "darling child". After the neutrality with which Maddy was used to being treated at school, it was very disturbing, but at least Maddy was able to persuade her into teaching mainly the subjects that Maddy liked.

Her mother and father were distinctly bewildered by the sudden turn of events, and Maddy could not make this out.

"But you *knew* I was going to be an actress, didn't you?"

"Well – yes, dear, but not quite so soon, and not on the films –"

To her parents this seemed even more outlandish than the stage, now that they had got used to the idea that the stage was to be Sandra's career. Sandra at first had been rather shaken by her little sister's piece of luck and pretended to look down on the films, but soon her curiosity could not be held in check and she went down to the location and enrolled as an extra. The work, though hard, was intriguing, and she was never tired of seeing Maddy treated as the "little star".

"You *will* look after Maddy down there," her mother pleaded.

Sandra tried to explain that what with Miss Garrard, Van Velden, Rodney, Denny Dent, Peggy, and all the other assistant directors looking after Maddy to a certain extent, her presence was rather unnecessary.

On the days Maddy was not needed she went to school as usual, and all her friends told her how lucky she was to escape school so often. After a while Maddy began to find school quite restful compared with a day on the set.

At first Van Velden patted himself on the back at finding a child so easy to handle. Her Blue Door training stood her in good stead, but as the character of Elizabeth of Fennymead became clearer to her she began to disagree with the script very often. One day, while running over a scene before shooting, Maddy rebelled.

"No," she said. "I can't say that. It sounds slushy. I'm sorry."

Van Velden expostulated, "But vot is wrong with it? In every film ze child she say, 'Don't cry, uncle, plis don't cry'."

"Yes," agreed Maddy, "and that's exactly why *I'm* not going to say it. And for another thing – Lord Moulcester wouldn't have cried – he'd just have got into a rage, and anyhow, even if he did cry, Elizabeth wouldn't have remarked on it."

Van Velden groaned. "Goot heffings, child, who directs this picture, you or me?"

Miss Garrard, who hovered nervously on the outskirts, pleaded, "Maddy, don't be difficult, there's a little darling."

Maddy withered her with a glance and turned again to Van Velden. "But don't you see – I can't say that line. It's Shirley Temple, not me. Oh, please cut it out, Mr. Van Velden. I'll look at him in a sympathetic sort of way, if you like, but I can't say – that awful line!"

Van Velden writhed in his chair with anger. "There I am. Alvays it happen the same when one try to work with a newcomer of no experience. I shall go now and drink a cup of coffee. Ver' hot it will be and ver' strong. Then perhaps we try to vork once more. Break, everyone!"

In the canteen while Maddy was drinking as little as possible of the milk Miss Garrard was pressing upon her, Felicity came up.

"I say, Felicity," said Maddy. "Don't you think I was right to refuse that line?"

"In one way, yes, dear," said Felicity, "I think you were – if it offended your aesthetic sensibilities."

Maddy giggled. "Oo-er! Where do I keep them?"

Felicity laughed and tried to explain. "Well, if it made you curl up inside to have to say it, you were quite right; but on the other hand, an actress should be able to recite the multiplication table and make it sound interesting."

Maddy was rather subdued. "I hadn't thought of that."

Felicity said, "You should have heard some of the lines I've had to say in awful plays I've done in repertory. Once I had to say, 'Lean your weary head on me, father. I will be your little comforter!' "

Maddy choked into her milk and spilt it conveniently on the floor. "Well," she admitted, "my line is certainly not as bad as that –"

"I should have a shot at it," Felicity advised.

"I know what," compromised Maddy, "I'll put my hand on his arm and say, 'Don't.' Will that do?"

"You'll feel much prouder of yourself if you actually say the line and get it to come over properly."

"All right. You win," sighed Maddy. The loud-speaker in the canteen boomed, "Everyone on the set, please," and hurrying out, Maddy approached Van Velden. "Hullo," she said. "Did you have a nice cup of coffee?"

"It is too hot," Van Velden told her unhappily. "My tonk it burn."

"Oh, I *am* sorry!" said Maddy. "But listen, Mr. Van Velden. I'll say your line. Felicity says I ought to."

Van Velden was overjoyed and kissed her warmly on both cheeks. For the rest of the day Maddy acted like an angel.

At first it had seemed to her that acting was the last thing to be considered in this film business. The set, the costumes, the camera angles all seemed to receive much more attention. It was only in the last few seconds before a shot was rehearsed or taken that Van Velden would draw her aside and try to explain with much waving of hands how he wanted it.

"It is *here* you must feel it!" he would insist, pointing to the region of his heart on the rather grubby woollen jumper he always wore.

"But I don't feel it there," disagreed Maddy. "I feel it here!" and she clasped her tummy. "When I'm excited I feel all bubbly, and when I'm unhappy I feel all heavy, and it's always *here*."

"Ach, I care not if you feel it in your littlest toe, only that you feel it somewhere!"

Felicity was lovely to act with.

"You make me feel as if I'm on the stage," Maddy told her, which Felicity rightly took as a great compliment.

Russell Durrant was quite easy to play with too, but Michael Strong, who played the uncle, was such a grand person that Maddy was rather in awe of him. She could never quite get over the fact that she used to go to the cinema to see his films, and once had had a photo of him pinned over her bed. Somehow it seemed an impertinence to be acting with him. He was much older than she had thought, and rather conscious of being a personage. Sometimes there were people hanging round the gates of the fields to get his autograph when he left, and when Maddy saw that some of them were girls from her school she felt ashamed somehow. It didn't seem right that she should be rolling off in her private car with Jo, the cheery driver, while they were lingering waiting for just a glimpse of "the film people".

The first thing that made her realize how things were changed was the attitude of Sally, her best friend at school.

They had always sat next to each other, ever since the First Form, but after a whole week of shooting she returned to find that Sally had moved to the other side of the classroom.

"Hi! Sal!" she yelled. "You come back over here where you belong!"

But Sally had tossed her head and replied, "Don't you order me about, Madelaine Fayne, even if you are a film star. I don't like sitting next to an empty desk when you're not here, and I can't say I'm so keen on sitting next to you when you *are* here, nowadays."

Maddy went home very puzzled and told Sandra.

"Don't worry," said Sandra. "I expect she's envious. She feels the film has taken you right away from her. But she'll soon come round when she gets used to the idea of your being in it. You haven't been showing off, have you?"

"No!" avowed Maddy, "not a bit. Not as much as I used to when I had nothing to show off about. I can't understand it."

"Success has its drawbacks," said Sandra wisely.

"I haven't *been* a success yet," cried Maddy. "I wish people wouldn't say things like that."

It was a letter from the rest of the Blue Door Theatre Company that finally put Maddy on her feet again.

"We want to let you know," they wrote, "that we are constantly thinking of you and keeping our fingers crossed. We are madly envious, and we know you won't let the Blue Door Theatre down."

"Now that," reflected Maddy, "is the right sort of envy!" and forgot all her troubles in writing them a long letter describing film life in great detail.

MADDY STORMS A CASTLE

One morning, after a rest of four days, Maddy was being driven in through the gates of the location when an extraordinary sight met her eyes. She cried out to Jo, the driver, "What on earth is that?"

"Looks like 'Atters Castle to me," he replied.

A new set had been constructed. It was a very bad reproduction of Fennymead Castle with many little additions and flights of fancy that completely out-Hollywooded any of Hollywood's worst efforts. Maddy ran over to the group of people who were surveying it doubtfully.

"It looks like something out of 'Snow-white' gone wrong," said Rodney with distaste. "I don't know what Van Velden is thinking of."

"And why try to improve on the original architecture?" demanded Felicity. "It's perfect as it stands."

Van Velden came up beaming. "Goot-morning, goot-morning! And how do you like my castle, yes?"

"We don't!" said Maddy flatly. "I can't think why you had to build one when you've got the real thing just over there."

"But we haf not ze real thing. Zat is ze back-draw!"

explained Van Velden. "Ze man who lives there nothing will have to do with us. I send him whisky. He drink it. I send him cigars. He smoke them. But he will not answer my letters. But Van Velden will not be squashed on. No." He made a sweeping gesture. "He build a better one."

"It's a very nice castle," began Felicity tactfully –

But Maddy broke in, "It's not a very nice castle. It's a terrible castle. And if you think I'm going to act in the same film with it you're very much mistaken." An exclamation of horror went round. "I'm acting in the real castle and nowhere else," went on Maddy, pink in the face with determination. "That awful thing will spoil the whole film. It's all right for you, Mr. Van Velden. I expect you'll go on making films all your life, and one ruined one does not matter, but this is probably the only one I'll ever make. So it's going to be a good one."

Van Velden tore at his pallid hair. "Most we haf all this once more? Ach, child, you are my evil spirit. Rodney, why did you ever bring this creature into my unfortunate life? At effery turn a headache she gif me. I am despairing –"

Rodney tried to be helpful. "You know, Maddy, it will probably look much better on the screen. You'd be surprised how awful most sets look close to."

"And the public won't know that it's not exactly like the real thing. They'll probably love it," Felicity put in.

Peggy said to Maddy persuasively, "Don't annoy poor Mr. Van Velden. He's got a headache. Run along to your dresser now. You want the sequence in night clothes, don't you, Mr. Van Velden?"

"Yes, plis, thank you. But first, Maddy, plis step inside my castle. You will see how extraordinary and how luffly it is. Not only do we use ze front, but inside there are rooms also. It is just as a real castle."

Maddy said calmly, "I am not going to step inside your horrible old castle. I am not going to put on my ridiculous night clothes. I am going home to clean out my goldfish pond." She turned to the driver of the car. "Home please, Jo."

"You are not to drive her a step!" roared Van Velden.

Jo looked from one to another in bewilderment.

"O.K. then. I shall walk," said Maddy. "You can send for me when you have got permission to use the castle from Lord Moulcester." She turned and made for the lane that led to the main road. She walked quickly, trying not to realize how rash she had been. After a few minutes she heard running footsteps behind her, and turning saw that Rodney was following her.

"Hi! Wait for me!" he cried. "I'm rather good with goldfish. How many have you got?"

"Well, I *had* six," Maddy told him. "But one of them was a cannibal. I've only got one now."

"And that's the cannibal, I suppose?"

"Yes. I call him Robinson Crusoe."

"It ought to be Man Friday, surely," said Rodney.

"Why? He wasn't a cannibal."

"Nor was Robinson Crusoe."

"I didn't say he was."

"Oh, don't let's quarrel," said Rodney.

"And I'm not coming back to act in that jerry-built castle whatever you say!" shouted Maddy firmly.

"You amaze me!" said Rodney. "You really do. Why, there are a thousand children who would give their ears to be you – to play such a wonderful part as this – and yet you seem to be doing your utmost to get thrown out."

Maddy kicked a stone along the ground for a little and then said, "You don't understand. You never worked in the Blue

Door Theatre. Before all the others went to Dramatic School and we used to give shows. They weren't very grand, but only the best that we could manage was good enough for us. If we wanted something really old we'd go and borrow it from an antique shop." She giggled reminiscently. "They usually sent me to do the asking." She suddenly stopped dead and turned to him.

"Rodney, I've got an idea. Once when we wanted a spinning-wheel I went and persuaded an antique dealer to lend us one. Well, now I want Fennymead Castle, so why shouldn't I go and persuade Lord Moulcester to let us use it?"

"Don't be silly!" said Rodney. "If he won't see Van Velden who sends him whisky and cigars, why should he see you?"

"Well," explained Maddy, "Van Velden obviously *wants* something, but I'm just an innocent little girl walking through his grounds making daisy chains, or something."

"And I suppose," jeered Rodney, "you'll find him in tears and say, 'Don't cry, Uncle, please don't cry'."

But Maddy was carried away with her idea. "I think I'm going to do it, Rodney. If only I knew more about Lord Moulcester, though. I'm sure he's not a moustache-twirling villain like his ancestor in the film. He's probably quite ordinary. He might even be interested in goldfish. You never know. Should I offer him Robinson Crusoe to add to his collection, do you think?"

Rodney laughed. "If Robinson Crusoe is all that you say, it would only serve to deplete his collection, I should think."

"Yes," agreed Maddy. "That's a pity. I might be able to house-train Robinson Crusoe first –"

"But you don't even know that Lord Moulcester likes goldfish," pointed out Rodney. "He might be allergic to them."

"Oh, I wouldn't let anyone ill-treat Robinson Crusoe."

"Stupid. I mean he might detest goldfish."

"Oh, I see."

They walked in silence towards the town. Suddenly Rodney said, "I say! Look at this old dame coming along here. What a peach of a hat! An absolute market garden on top of it."

Maddy looked. "Why, it's Mrs. Potter-Smith!" And I'm allergic to her! But she might know something about Lord Moulcester. Watch me pump her."

"Well, well, well!" cried Mrs. Potter-Smith when she was still many yards away, "if it isn't our little film star. Quite a celebrity now, aren't we?"

"Good-morning, Mrs. Potter-Smith!" said Maddy politely. "Are you going down to watch the filming?"

Mrs. Potter-Smith laughed artificially, showing her false teeth. "Good gracious me, no! I just happened to be taking my morning constitutional in this direction. No, I can't say that films interest me much. I don't know why it is – But Maddy, you haven't introduced me to your little friend. Is he an actor too?"

"Oh, no!" said Maddy, "he's just a musician."

"Just a musician! And what better! Now I have always been so interested in music –"

Maddy broke in with, "Oh, by the way, Mrs. Potter-Smith, do you happen to know Lord Moulcester?"

"Know him?" She arched her eyebrows until they disappeared under the brim of her ridiculous hat. "My dear we shared the same cradle!"

Maddy giggled.

Mrs. Potter-Smith put in hurriedly, "I mean, we might have done, had we been babies at the same time, but, of course, he is many years older than I, oh yes, many many years. Such a sad story, I always think." She sighed sentimentally. "Living all alone in that draughty old castle with only one servant. And he was such a gay, handsome young man in his day."

"He certainly seems a bad-tempered old buffer now. He won't let us use his castle in the film."

"Won't he," said Mrs. Potter-Smith. "Won't he indeed! Well now, I think I can explain that. When he was a young man, about twenty or so, he ran away from university to go on the stage. He joined some touring company and went all over the place for a year or so playing in the small provincial towns. But then when the cinemas were started business was so bad that the company had to be disbanded, and Ernie –"

"Who?"

"His name is Ernest, but I always used to call him Ernie," she giggled self-consciously. "So you see, Ernie came home and buried himself at Fennymead, seeing hardly any one."

"Oh," said Maddy, with dawning hope. "So he's been an actor –"

"Just listen to me running on – what a little chatterbox I am!" giggled Mrs. Potter-Smith. "You must forgive me, Mr. Musician. Oh –" She opened her eyes very wide, "Now I wonder – You know it's a very small world, isn't it? As it happens, I am looking for a musician. You see, from time to time our Ladies' Institute, of which I am the organiser, gives little concerts, mainly run by me, if I may say so, and one of the chief items is always a little song by myself. Well, now, unfortunately, the curate who always plays for me has got measles and so I wondered if –"

Rodney was speechless with horror.

Maddy put in hurriedly, "Oh, Rodney only plays swing, Mrs. Potter-Smith, but of course if you're going to sing 'In the Mood' or 'Alexander's Ragtime Band', he'd be delighted."

Mrs. Potter-Smith considered this quite seriously and then said, "Well, no, dear. I had planned to sing a jolly little thing – How does it go?" She warbled in a falsetto voice:

> " 'Come follow, follow, follow
> The merry, merry pipes of Pan –'

Anything with a little fantasy is always so popular, you know – Well, I'm sorry you can't manage it – but we can't all appreciate the classics, can we?"

"No," agreed Rodney with fervour. "We can't."

"I must be getting along," said Mrs. Potter-Smith at last. "Cheery-bye, kiddies!"

"What an incredible woman!" said Rodney.

But Maddy only walked in silence with a determined gleam in her eye.

For the next few days the situation was at a deadlock. Van Velden continued to bombard Lord Moulcester with gifts and Maddy with letters. At last came one saying that unless Maddy turned up on the location next day she would lose the part.

"I cannot understand you!" ranted Sandra. "To throw over such a heaven-sent opportunity over such a small point –"

But Maddy continued to eat her cornflakes with an enigmatic smile.

"Well, what are you going to do?" demanded Sandra. "I'm going down this morning, so you'd better make up your mind and I'll take a note to Van Velden."

"Don't bother!" said Maddy airily. "I may come down this morning – and I may not. It all depends –"

Sandra took hold of her by the shoulders and shook her. "Maddy! What are you planning? You've got something up your sleeve, haven't you?"

Maddy opened her eyes innocently. "Up my sleeve? What *do* you mean?" She shook herself free and ran to the door.

"Where are you going?" cried Sandra.

"Visiting!" laughed Maddy, as she jumped on her bicycle. "Yes. I'm going to visit Lord Moulcester. You can expect me when you see me," and she whizzed down the road.

When she reached the castle grounds she got off her bike and hid it in a ditch. Then she crawled through the hedge. Among the trees it was dark and still. Occasionally she caught a glimpse of the greyness of the castle.

"Lord Moulcester," she murmured, "here I come."

8

ENTER LORD MOULCESTER

It was quite a long way to the castle, and Maddy threaded her way through the trees trying to make up her mind what she would say when she met Lord Moulcester. She had never spoken to a lord before. From somewhere near at hand she heard the sound of an axe, and pushing her way through some brambles she found herself in a little clearing, where an old man was cutting down a tree.

Maddy liked seeing other people work and she was rather warm, so she sat down on the grass for a rest and watched him. He was very thin and bony, and had a little white goatee beard. His coat was very old and had leather on the elbows.

"What a shame," thought Maddy, "to make such an old man cut down trees. Lord Moulcester *must* be a horrible person." After a little while she said in a friendly manner, "It's going to take you an awful long time to get that tree down, isn't it? Why don't you take it easy? I don't see the point of cutting trees down all over the place. It's much more fun just to sit under them and think about things like I do. But I suppose if old Lord Moulcester tells you to, you have to. Is he really a horrid old thing? I've heard he is. And if he makes a poor old man like you cut down trees all day, he must be. And that's an awful pity, because, you see, I've come to ask him a favour."

The old man put down his axe and looked at her. His face was so thin that his cheekbones stuck out and his eyes seemed to burn very brightly.

"And what might that be?" he asked.

"Well, it's rather a long story," said Maddy. "Do you mind if I tell you? I know what, I'll practise on you so that when I meet Lord Moulcester I'll be able to melt his heart of stone."

The wood-cutter seemed amused. "Fire away!" he said. "I'm listening."

Maddy jumped up in order to give her story its full dramatic value. "When I see Lord Moulcester," she began, "I shall say, 'Lord Moulcester, you see before you a humble girl whose life you have ruined by your selfishness –' "

"Good Lord!" exclaimed the wood-cutter.

But Maddy would not be deterred. "And then he'll say, 'Speak, child, and I will hear your plea.' So then I'll tell him the whole story."

"And what is the story?" The wood-cutter sounded interested.

Maddy stopped being dramatic. "It may sound silly to you. I mean, living out here in the woods, worldly ambitions must seem rather rot to you, but do try to understand. You see I want to be an actress. It's the only thing I want, but I want it so much that it hurts. Some time ago I was having an opportunity to act in the Blue Door Theatre in Fenchester –"

"The Blue Door Theatre," repeated the old man. "I believe I read about it in the local paper. A whole lot of children or something, wasn't it?"

"Yes, that's right," said Maddy. "Oh, it was such fun. We always had some show or other to rehearse. And now I miss it so. All the others were old enough to go away to Dramatic School, and here I am, left in misery."

"And what has Lord Moulcester to do with it?"

"Well, you see, a little while ago I got the biggest chance of my life. I was chosen to play the part of Elizabeth of Fennymead in *Forsaken Crown* – that's the film about Fennymead –"

The wood-cutter attacked the tree again with vigour. "And what has that got to do with your ambitions as an actress?" he wanted to know.

"I see what you mean," said Maddy. "I know that there is very little real acting on the screen. But since I've been filming I've realized that an actress who can get things over on a noisy set surrounded by cameras and lighting effects, and with scenes chopped up into little bits, is much more clever than one on the stage, who has all the surroundings in her favour."

"How old are you, child?" asked the wood-cutter.

"Twelve. But I expect my sorrows have aged me."

"But tell me," he pursued, "how does all this affect Lord Moulcester?"

Maddy sighed. "Well, now I've been rather silly and spoilt my chances. You know Fennymead Castle?"

"Er – certainly."

"Well, you see, it comes into the film –"

"So I gather," said the old man sourly.

"And Lord Moulcester won't let us use the real castle. So they've built an awful phoney-looking imitation one. It's all plaster and wood, and not a bit like the real one. And so – I've refused to act in it."

"That surely is rather foolish?"

Maddy reflected that this old man spoke very nicely for a wood-cutter or a gamekeeper or whatever he was.

"Yes, I know it's foolish," admitted Maddy, "because in my heart of hearts I don't think that I shall ever be able to get round a selfish old pig like Lord Moulcester. And yet I'm not going to give in now, after I've wasted everyone's time for so long. I *must* get the use of the castle – or else give up my part. And it's *such* a lovely part."

"Tell me," said the wood-cutter, "why do you think Lord Moulcester should allow his castle to be overrun by these film people?"

"Well, I should think he has some family pride, hasn't he?" demanded Maddy.

"He has indeed," said the old man gravely.

"Then I shouldn't think he'd like people to think that he lived in a tatty castle like the imitation one when really it's as beautiful as it is."

"You certainly have made a point." Her listener dropped his axe and put his hands in the pockets of his weather-beaten coat.

"It's so silly of him not to co-operate," went on Maddy. "He's just the person we need. You see, Van Velden is a Dutchman –"

"You surprise me."

"So he can't be expected to have the same historical sort of feeling for England as an Englishman. He knows an awful lot, and he's got plenty of what he calls 'authenticity men', but they're no good. Why they didn't even know that Elizabeth of Fennymead was a little girl."

"I'm surprised to find that they are playing her at the correct age," said the wood-cutter.

Maddy said proudly, "Oh, that was me and the Bishop. We discovered that."

The wood-cutter was surprised. "So the Bishop is interested in the film?"

"Oh yes. He's not interested in films usually, but he says that as it's about our town and ancestors it's important. And after all, Lord Moulcester should be particularly interested because it's about his great, great, great – oh ever so may greats – grandfather."

"I think," said the wood-cutter slowly, "that if he did take an interest in the film it would be more because of the sincerity of the little leading lady than anything."

"Do you?" asked Maddy overjoyed. "Then you think it might be some good if I saw him?"

"I do indeed."

"Then please take me to him," pleaded Maddy. "Please."

The wood-cutter shook his head. "I fear he is rather busy at the moment, but I may be able to persuade him to talk to you later on."

"But it's so urgent, Mr. Woodcutter, I can't hold out much longer without losing the part. And oh, I do want to play Elizabeth. She's so nice. Why does Lord Moulcester have to be so much against films?"

"Because his own career was ruined by them, and because of their complete disregard for the accuracies and beauties of history," said the old man heavily.

"But there's no need for him to stand by and see someone else's career ruined, is there? And if only he'd come and *help* us with the accuracies and beauties, everyone would be happy. Oh, please see what you can do."

"I will, my child. Now you must return to your film company and I'll see what I can do. If Lord Moulcester can be persuaded, he'll be with you before long."

Maddy jumped for joy. "Oh, thank you, thank you! You dear old man! If you hadn't got a beard I would kiss you. I must run now. Oh, *won't* they be surprised?"

Van Velden sat in his office surrounded by his underlings. He was too dispirited even to drink coffee.

"Then it is decisioned, yes? We leaf Fenchester, return to ze studios, rebuild ze castle, and test all our starlets under contract till we find a new Elizabeth."

There were murmurs of dispirited agreement.

"Poor Maddy!" said Felicity. "I can't bear to think how upset she'll be."

"All is her own fault," said Van Velden. "But I cannot help to be sorry. Alvays a curse there has been on this film. A most unfortunate man am I."

There was silence while everyone hoped that Van Velden would not burst into tears. In the distance came Maddy's voice very faintly, "Mr. Van Velden! Mr. Van Velden!" She appeared in the doorway breathless and triumphant. "It's happened! I think he's coming – any minute now –" she gasped.

"What on earth are you talking about?" demanded Denny Dent.

"Lord Moulcester is coming to see you, Mr. Van Velden. I saw an old gamekeeper or something of his who seems to know him very well, and he said that he's going to persuade him to come down here."

"Goot heffings!" cried Van Velden. "Child, I bless you! And now I haf just decisioned to give you the bag and return to London, but now all will be well." He hurried out to the lot and yelled through the mike, "Efferyone hold efferything efferywhere. We do not go. We stay. Lord Moulcester comes to visit with us. Very busy and very happy we must seem."

There was a murmur of delight from the technicians and extras and artistes, and everyone patted Maddy on the back until she was sore. Immediately they began to prepare for the shooting of a scene as Van Velden wished to make an impression of great industry. Maddy hastily changed into one of her prettiest dresses and everyone charged about madly, trying to appear "busy and happy" but with one eye on the path that led down the hill from the Fennymead woods. At last appeared a solitary figure, tall and rather bent.

"Cut!" cried Van Velden, and he and Maddy went forward to meet him.

"Oh!" exclaimed Maddy. "It's only the wood-cutter."

"No, no!" hissed Van Velden. "It is Lord Moulcester. A photo I haf seen. I know it is he!"

"It's the wood-cutter!"

"It is Lord Moulcester."

"It's the wood-cutter."

"My name is Moulcester," said the visitor, holding out his hand. "You, I believe, are Mr. Van Velden. Our little actress here I already know. In fact we have had a heart-to-heart talk this afternoon."

"Oh!" gasped Maddy. "If I'd known it was you."

Lord Moulcester laughed kindly, "I know. You would have told me that I saw before me a humble girl whose life I had ruined by my selfishness. No, my dear, your story was much more effective as told to the wood-cutter."

"And all the rude things I said about you!" wailed Maddy.

"I must apologise, Mr. Van Velden," he went on, "for my boorishness in not acknowledging your letters and gifts. Now I wish to make up for it by any assistance I can offer. If there are any details you wish to know of my family's history or my castle's history –"

"Zis is too true to be goot," said Van Velden. "I thank you. Come, sir, to my hut and ve vill talk."

"What about me?" asked Maddy.

"You? You may go and eat many sticky buns in the canteen."

"I need them," shouted Maddy, careering off to tell Sandra the latest dramatic news.

The interview with Lord Moulcester was most successful. He promised to check the script to see that facts were correct and to supply more details. But nothing was yet said about the castle. Finally Lord Moulcester asked permission to look over the location, and see a shot taken. He seemed intrigued by the cameras and all the technicalities.

"Well, I'm blessed!" he kept repeating. "Well, I'm blessed!" But the sight of the imitation castle moved him to disgust. "And how much would be wasted if you were to scrap that set?" he asked at last.

Van Velden's eyes gleamed. "It cost, of course, a lot of money, but all that we would waste we would also gain."

"H'm!" said Lord Moulcester. "Well –" Then at length, "I suppose there's really no reason why you shouldn't film in the castle. Providing that you don't blackguard my illustrious ancestor too much. I certainly would prefer to have my home overrun by these young things in corduroy than to allow an atrocity like that set to appear to the public as Fennymead Castle."

Van Velden shut his eyes to realize the portent of these words. Then he wrung Lord Moulcester by the hand. "My lord," he said. "You are a real English gentleman."

"So I should hope," mumbled Lord Moulcester. "So I should hope."

Van Velden leaped to the microphone like an agile elephant. "That is all for today, everybody, plis. No artistes required tomorrow. We are moving to the castle." There was a burst of cheering from the extras. "Tomorrow we strike ze set, plis, and survey ze castle. Check in on Friday morning ze usual time, plis. Good-bye and God bless efferyone," he added expansively.

Although no artistes were called for the next day, Maddy, Felicity, and Sandra made their way to the castle. It was grey and massively built, with the grace and dignity of extreme age. Inside it was damp and draughty, but every corner invited a special shot to be taken. Maddy ran about excitedly shouting to the cameraman, who was a minute little Russian with a stammer that made him completely incomprehensible. "Look, look! This corridor will do for the scene with Felicity. We can walk right down the whole length of it." The cameraman was twisting himself into knots looking through his cupped hands to judge camera angles.

"There's some dungeons!" cried Maddy. "Oh, we must have a scene in a dungeon. I'll ask Hans to get one written in."

Felicity and Sandra admired the architecture together.
"How lucky," said Felicity, "that it hasn't been restored or renovated too obviously." She squeezed Sandra's arm delightedly. "It's going to be good now, isn't it?" she said.

"Yes," agreed Sandra smiling, "I think it is."

And Maddy, who was running wildly round the battlements, *knew* it was going to be.

THE POTTER-SMITH REBELLION

It was the first day of shooting at the real castle and some exterior scenes were being retaken. Lord Moulcester looked on with great interest, and everyone told him how lovely the castle looked in the sunlight.

"At last, at last!" cried Van Velden, "my troubles all are over. A new man am I, and a masterpiece shall we make."

Everyone worked very conscientiously to make up for all the lost time, and take after take went smoothly. It was towards the end of the lunch break that trouble appeared in the bulky form of Mrs. Potter-Smith. Everyone was stretched out dozing peacefully on the banks of the shallow moat that surrounded the castle when the silence of the afternoon was shattered by her piercing tones. She had discovered Van Velden in a deck-chair with his beret tilted over his eyes, snoring slightly.

"Ah! So this is the great man I have heard so much about. Well, well, well! How glad I am to meet you. My name is Potter-Smith, you know, and my nephew, Jacky, has a friend who works in your studios, so he said that if I came to see you, you would give me a part in your film."

Van Velden surveyed her podgy features with distaste. "I'm sorry, plis –" he began.

"Of course I'm not just a little amateur crashing in. I have acted ever since I could walk. Before, even. I'm sure there must be some nice little part just suited to me."

Rodney whispered to Maddy, who was watching this little scene delightedly, "I say, couldn't we use her in the kitchen scene? She'd make a nice ham strung from the ceiling."

"Of course," continued Mrs. Potter-Smith, "I really go in more for the musical side of things. Now don't you think it would be rather dinky if the film opened with someone playing a spinet and singing some quaint old folk tune? I'm sure I could do that most touchingly."

Van Velden rose and straightened his beret, then went very close to her so that the cherries on her hat dangled under his nose. "Madame!" he said. "Since you insist. One of the rabble who storm ze castle you may be. Go now to the tent marked 'Extras' and fill in a form – two forms – as many forms as you vish – but leaf me alone, plis thank you. I am busy man."

Mrs. Potter-Smith heaved with indignation. "Well, I never did. I certainly did not expect such treatment here. An extra, indeed! Good afternoon!"

Van Velden sighed and raised his eyes to heaven. Mrs. Potter-Smith approached Maddy.

"Oh, Maddy, dear," she whispered. "Where is the tent marked 'Extras'?"

"Over there." Maddy pointed it out. "I'm so glad you're joining us."

"Little hypocrite!" whispered Rodney in her ear.

They were idyllic summer days. The shooting had taken on a new lease of life since the move to the castle. Even the weather kept fine for them, and every day Maddy was on the set at ten, working like a Trojan until four or five. Van Velden and all the technicians began to catch the sun and soon looked as brown as berries. Even Van Velden's woolly jumper of uncertain colour gave place to a shirt of gay yellow check. After the day's work was over, Maddy, Felicity, Rodney, and Sandra would cycle down to Browcliffe for a swim. Sitting on the cliff top they would discuss the film, acting in general, and Rodney's music. He was turning it out fast now, and at odd moments would approach one with a glazed look in his eye humming "Da-da-di-de – da-da-di-da – How's that for the opening theme?"

These expeditions to Browcliffe were almost the happiest times for Maddy, for now the success or failure of the film had reached enormous proportions in her mind, and while she was acting she was haunted by the fear that she was not being good enough. "Was I really all right today?" she would demand of Sandra. "I'm not looking for compliments, but if I was awful please tell me so." And Sandra would give a detailed criticism in the fairest possible terms.

Sometimes if she were not needed in the afternoon she and Rodney would take a busman's holiday and go to the cinema. She found that her interest in the cinema had increased enormously, as now she had not only the story and acting to enjoy, but all the technical details were no secret from her.

"Nice spot of panning, that," she would whisper to Rodney.

"Yes, but listen to this atrocious piece of violin music."

"Sh!" their neighbours would hiss so that they collapsed into giggles and then went to have tea at the milk bar.

Fenchester was a changed town. Every hotel and boarding house was crowded with "those film people", who were to be seen returning from the Fennymead fields every evening, sometimes still wearing their vivid technicolour make-ups. Some of the extras were Londoners especially brought down, and some local people had been brought in to make up the numbers. There was slight friction between the two groups because their pay was equal, whereas the Londoners considered that they should receive extra for their board and lodging.

"Oh gosh!" cried Denny Dent, one night after the pay-off. "It's as bad as trying to run a kindergarten."

"What's the matter now?" asked Peggy.

"They're grumbling because there's some woman who says she's doing this voluntarily and not accepting her pay as she doesn't need it. And they hold that she ought to be turned off to make room for someone who needs work."

Peggy ran her eye down a list. "Oh, yes. That must be the awful Smith woman. Yes, look – Potter-Smith. She hasn't collected her pay for a long time. What had we better do with it?"

"Ask her if she wants it, and if she doesn't, give it to charity, I suppose. It is a shame, though. And if we're not careful we shall be in for another trade union row."

"Let's hope we've had enough rows on this job!" said Peggy.

Mrs. Potter-Smith was making herself known in other ways. She was consistently late on the set, arriving just as the crowd had been grouped satisfactorily without her.

"Oh, Mr. Director!" she would cry. "What do I have to do? Where do I go?"

"One day," sighed Denny, "I shall tell her where to go in no uncertain terms."

It was in the crowd dressing-room that Mrs. Potter-Smith excelled herself. Now that they were shooting in the castle it was decided that it was a waste of time for the extras to dress in their original tent in the fields and trail up to the castle. Therefore Lord Moulcester had allowed them to use the basements. The men's room was large and quite airy, but the one used by the women was smaller and badly ventilated. The representatives of the crowd women, however, had reported to Van Velden that they were quite willing to use it to save precious time. After they had been installed for about a week, Mrs. Potter-Smith, who had by far the largest share of dressing-table space, began to grumble.

"I don't know, I'm sure," she said, rubbing foundation into her fleshy face, "how they expect us to make ourselves look decent in a chicken coop like this. No elbow-room –" she dug her neighbour sharply in the ribs as she wielded a hair brush, "and as for the ventilation – well, I wonder more people don't faint on the set. Fancy, three again today – really, the conditions are a scandal. I should like to write up about it."

"Where to?" someone inquired.

"Anywhere!" said Mrs. Potter-Smith stoutly. "Really I wonder why you poor dears do it for so little money. Of course, I'm only doing it for Mr. Van Velden. 'Mrs. Potter-Smith,' he said, 'the film would be *nothing* without you.' But really – if I had known what the conditions were to be like –"

"Blimey!" said one of the London women, " 'Ark at 'er! Conditions, indeed! You should 'er seen some of the studios we worked in in the early days, eh, Gert?" She turned to a friend for confirmation. "No runnin' water! No nothing! And 'undreds of us 'erded in like sheep. Lor' no! This place is a picnic. A proper picnic it is. Out in the country. No gettin' up early to travel miles 'n miles. Coo! You oughtn'ter grumble!"

But all the same, some of the less hardy local people, who regarded Mrs. Potter-Smith as a rather superior personage, agreed with her and joined in with their grumbles. It started with the subject of the dressing-rooms, then spread to pay, hours of working, and the food provided by the canteen. Van Velden would take no notice of the rumours of complaint that reached him.

"Grumble? Of course they grumble! What else to do all day have they but grumble? All extras grumble always. It is nothink."

"I don't know!" said Denny Dent. "I don't know, I'm sure!" He wrinkled his handsome forehead.

"There must be no troubles now," asserted Van Velden, "for on Thursday M'Kinnon, Goldberg, and Evans from the Company Trust visit with us. By then I hope that we may shoot ze big scene when ze crowd storm ze castle. It must be goot, for I have to demand of the Trust a bigger grant to cover all this time we haf wasted. If they do not agree –" He shook his head sadly.

"Shall I fetch you your aspirins?" asked Maddy, noticing that he looked doleful.

"No, my leetle one. But listen, plis. On Thursday three men come here to see us work. They are from the board who provide the money for this film. Already we have spent too much and now more I must demand. They may grant it – and they may not. You can help. Ver' charming and hard-working you must be. You must make them see how worthy a film this is."

"I'll be as sweet as sugar!" promised Maddy, "just like when the inspectors come round at school."

But on the Wednesday their hopes were dashed. Sandra, nearly in tears, approached Van Velden during the tea break. "Excuse me, Mr. Van Velden. May I see you a minute?" Sandra was a favourite of Van Velden's. She never caused trouble.

"Yes, yes, my dear. Sit down here." He drew up a canvas chair beside his own and continued to sip his coffee noisily.

"The extras are planning to strike!" gasped Sandra. "I feel awful at sneaking to you beforehand like this, but I know how important tomorrow is."

"But what is wrong?"

"Oh, everything! That wretched Mrs. Potter-Smith is at the head of it. She's worked them up to a pitch about the dressing-rooms, and now some of the others are going to demand not only more pay for those who are not resident in Fenchester, but equal pay for men and women!"

Van Velden crumpled his face up like a baby who is about to cry. "No more, plis! I can stand no more – Denny! Peggy! Come here, I beg you!" He told them the news.

"I knew it!" cried Denny. "There's been something in the air ever since that snake in female clothing appeared." The snake in female clothing was at that moment haranguing the crowd.

"So now I say, stand up for yourselves and your rights. If you strike Van Velden will soon realize how necessary you are to him. This does not affect me personally. I have no axe to grind. I come amongst you as a stranger. But justice is the Potter-Smith motto –"

"We must do something quickly!" said Denny, eyeing the turbulent groups that were arguing and gesticulating all around them.

Maddy, who had been hovering near the directors, said, "I've got an idea." No one listened so she stood on a chair. "I've got an idea!" she repeated. "Tell them now, this minute, that they won't be wanted any more. That'll shake them."

"But we must haf them!" groaned Van Velden.

"Yes, of course. But then at pay-off tell them that owing to an extra grant from the Trust we can afford to keep them on a bit longer."

"But suppose the grant we do not get?"

"We've *got* to!" Maddy stamped her foot. "Of course we've got to. Go on, Mr. Van Velden. Risk it. If you won't, I will."

"Denny!" said Van Velden weakly. "Do like she say. I cannot now spik to anyones."

Denny sprang to the mike just as Mrs. Potter-Smith approached bearing a banner. It was a large white handkerchief on which had been inscribed with grease paint. "Justice for the down-trodden extras!"

"Take notice, extras please!" shouted Denny, in the nick of time. "This is your last day's shooting. No more work at all. Thank you everyone very much." A cry of horror went up. One of the women turned angrily to Mrs. Potter-Smith.

"There you are, you silly great porpoise! You and your strikes. You don't need your pay, don't you? Well, we do. Four months' work we'd been promised on this, before you began all this strikin' rot. So now it's back to London and tramping round the agents for most of us. And I've got four kids to keep." All the arrogance of the crowd was gone. They talked together in subdued voices.

"Might get some chorus work, dearie –"

"Think I'll go back to charring. At least it's steady work –"

At the pay-off Denny announced, "Good news, folks. Owing to an unexpected grant from the Company Trust we shall be able to use you a little bit longer. On the set same time as usual tomorrow, please." The Castle grounds rang with cheers. All thoughts of the strike were forgotten. Van Velden subsided into his chair and let out his belt a few holes.

"Maddy!" he said. "Sometimes it seem to me you are more nuisance than you are worth, but now I know your worth is more than you nuisance."

Maddy beamed happily.

Messrs. M'Kinnon, Goldberg, and Evans had thoroughly enjoyed the lunch in the artistes' canteen. Van Velden had seen to it that there was plenty of everything, and now they were parked in comfortable chairs in the sun, smoking fat cigars. All was set for the shooting of one of the big scenes – the castle stormed by the villagers. This particular scene had been rehearsed all the morning, and Van Velden yearned to do it in only one take to show his efficiency and economy and the ability of his little star. There was an air of tension as the cameras and sound were checked.

"Action!" Maddy stepped out on to the balcony before the roaring crowd. It was her best moment. She felt larger than life. "What are all you people doing here?" she cried. "Don't you know my uncle has been wounded? How dare you disturb him when he is sleeping? Please go away at once –"

Suddenly something seemed to go wrong in the crowd. Mrs. Potter-Smith was pushing her way right up to the camera.

"Oh, stop a minute, please!" she cried. "My wig is all crooked."

"Cut! Get that woman off the set."

The take was ruined. Maddy burst into tears. With a cry of rage Rodney ran towards Mrs. Potter-Smith to clear her off the set. The ground sloped down towards the moat. He cannoned into her and she staggered back. There was a splash and a scream. Van Velden looked with agony in his eyes at the three Trust members. All three were snoring slightly in their chairs. He mopped his brow. The splash had woken Goldberg.

"Good effect that!" he murmured and slept again.

10

THE SUMMER IS OVER

The grant was allowed with no difficulty at all. Maddy bombarded all three of the Company Trust with such a battery of compliments, pleasantries, and endearing young charms that they were all completely conquered. They returned to London to report very favourably on the new starlet.

"Phew!" puffed Maddy as their car drove off. "That was a hard day's work!"

"You were simply killing me," Rodney told her. "I expected you to sprout dimples at any moment, and certainly to say, "Don't cry, Uncle, please don't cry.""

"Ver' goot!" commented Van Velden. "Once more my child, you save ze situations. But why, I ask you, do you not behave so to me? Zese smiles, zis sweet temper – it is amazink."

"Oh well," said Maddy, "I don't *want* anything from you."

"But now," said Van Velden, "there is something from you I want. And from all others in the company. Zat is – work! Work, work, work! Zis grant we haf and we must a move get on to finish before ze summer end. Understood, yes?"

At last the fates were kind to Van Velden and there were no disturbances. Scene after scene was taken and the film began to take shape. Several of the film magazines published "Candid Camera Photos" of the shooting and Maddy began to receive a sort of fan mail. These were mainly begging letters, and requests from tooth paste firms to use her name in their advertisements.

"Oh, *please* let me advertise 'Snow-white' tooth paste, Mr. Van Velden," she begged. "I've always wanted to –"

But Mr. Van Velden was adamant. "No!" he said. "No advertisink."

"But they'd pay me!" pleaded Maddy. "I could make some money."

Van Velden threw back his head and roared with laughter at this remark and then repeated it to Denny, who also laughed.

"What's the matter? What have I said that is so funny?" she wanted to know.

"Listen, kid, do you know how much we're putting in the bank for you every week?" said Denny.

"No," said Maddy. "Daddy deals with all that." When Denny told her how much she was none the wiser, for it was such a large sum that it meant nothing to her. She still received the same amount of pocket money, so her wealth did not affect her.

The new starlet was most thrilled by the gifts of clothes from London firms with requests to wear them for publicity photos or "public occasions". The only "public occasion" Maddy could think of was going to church on Sundays, and she didn't think that the Vicar would be very pleased if she turned up in the snappy orange play suit sent by a leading Bond Street firm. So these glamorous garments were hung up in her wardrobe waiting for the right occasion, while Maddy continued to wear her old linen frocks and shorts in which she could do acrobatics with objections from no one.

The summer wore on. Sandra had had another term at Dramatic School and returned for the holidays because of the film. Most of the crowd scenes were finished and the extras departed. Mrs. Potter-Smith had not appeared again since her involuntary swim in the moat, and therefore there had been less friction. Only a few scenes between Felicity, Maddy, Russell, and Michael Strong remained, and Maddy realized suddenly that the end of her filming days was in view.

"What next?" she thought. "What ever next?" The thought of returning to school in the autumn term filled her with horror. Van Velden explained to her that he would be unable to sign her up for another film until the results of this one had been seen. She began to try and make the days go more slowly by appreciating them. At odd moments she would think to herself, "Here I am, sitting in the artistes' canteen eating ice-cream. Felicity, Rodney, everyone is here – all being nice to me. And in a week or two they won't be here. And it will all be over." It seemed impossible. But soon there was only a few days' work left. One by one the people playing minor roles had departed, half sorry to leave, half glad to be returning to their homes. It was rather like the last days of term except that for Maddy there was nothing to be joyful about. Several times it seemed as if everything were finished, but when the "rushes" were seen in the little projection hut some small flaw was discovered, and there had to be some more takes. But inevitable the day came when Van Velden roared "Cut!" to the last take.

In order to celebrate, Lord Moulcester provided a sumptuous tea set out on trestle tables behind the castle. There were blackberries and cream and meringues, but Maddy was rather subdued. Everyone else was hilarious. Van Velden felt an immense relief that this undertaking had at last been completed after so many set-backs. Felicity looked forward to returning to her little flat and all her friends and, above all, to the stage. She was to appear in an autumn season of Shakespeare in London, playing Desdemona, Rosalind, and the Shrew, and already was hard at work learning her lines. Rodney had a fond mother and father to return to and a further contract with the same company. Sandra would soon be going back to Dramatic School once more. Even the little Russian cameraman was looking forward to seeing his wife and eleven children.

They sat late round the tables and the evening shadows grew longer. The technicians spoke nostalgically of all the home streets and pubs and cinemas that they would soon see again. Maddy got more and more depressed. After a while she realized that Lord Moulcester, too, had a long face. Perhaps he was feeling that he would miss them as well. She went and sat by him.

"I expect," she said, "that you'll be glad to have your castle to yourself again."

He shook his head slowly. "No," he said, "no, on the contrary, it will seem empty for the first time. I hadn't realized before what a difference young voices about the place can make."

"Oh, don't feel like that," said Maddy, "I'll come and visit you every week and make so much noise that you won't have a chance to feel lonely."

"Thank you, Maddy," he said, "that would help a lot." They sat in silence listening to the others making plans for the departure. Van Velden was driving Felicity, Russell, and Rodney up to town next day, and Denny and Peggy would stay behind to supervise the final clearing up and striking of the little encampment in the fields. At last Van Velden got up and shook hands with Lord Moulcester.

"Good-bye, my lord," he said, "and thank you many times for all you haf done. We hope to see you in London for the première." This had not been spoken of before.

"What about me?" said Maddy.

"You, of course, yes!" said Van Velden. "Your first public appearance it will be."

Maddy's heart lifted. Something to look forward to! Next day she went round to the hotel where Van Velden was staying to say good-bye. His long red sports car was standing outside with luggage on the back. Hans appeared, looking very smart in a suit all of the same colour for once. Even Rodney was spruced up a bit and seemed excited. They all said good-bye to her with affection and many "See-you-soons" and got into the car. The engine roared and it shot off down the road. Maddy waved until it was a red speck in the distance and the tears pricked in her throat. She stood there for a long time looking vacantly at the street, until a voice passing by floated to her.

"Look! There's Madelaine Fayne. You know – the film star!" Her face flushed as if she were guilty and she ran all the way home.

At lunch her father said, "Well, I can't help feeling glad that all this film business is over and you can settle down for a steady term at school with no upsets."

Maddy said nothing and looked very hard at her plate. Sandra was discussing what clothes she would take back to Dramatic School. Maddy regarded the blank future. Perhaps next holidays the Blue Doors *would* come home. They had all got jobs this summer, mainly in repertory, but Sandra had returned to see the finishing of the film. And now even she would be gone again. Maddy could hardly eat her pudding for emotion.

After lunch she went down to the Fennymead fields where Denny and Peggy were busy supervising the loading of several lorries and trucks with equipment. Maddy forgot her sorrows by fetching and carrying and getting gloriously dirty. She borrowed a pair of dungarees from one of the workmen and rolled them up so that the legs did not trail, but even then the seat was rather baggy. At last the lorries were loaded and they drove off. Maddy, with a burst of wit, had found some chalk and written "Just Married" on the back of each of the enormous vehicles.

"Gosh!" said Peggy. "What couldn't I do to a cup of tea!"

Just then Lord Moulcester appeared like a good fairy with a tray of tea and they sat on the grass and drank it. The remaining workmen came up and said, "All right to go now, sir?"

"Yes," said Denny, "off you go."

They touched their caps and said, "Good-bye, Miss" to Maddy, and even their departure made her sad.

"We'd better check up," said Peggy, and Maddy accompanied them on a last journey round the castle and grounds. Nothing was left behind. Costumes, properties, sets, and equipment had disappeared like magic. Everywhere seemed strangely empty. Lord Moulcester looked very much alone as he stood at the gateway of the drive and waved to them. Then he turned back to his castle where silence reigned as if it had never been banished.

"How about coming back to the hotel for dinner?" suggested Denny.

"Rather!" agreed Maddy. "I need it after all this hard work." They were too tired to talk much, but they ate a lot.

"I'll come down to the station and see you off tomorrow," promised Maddy.

Next morning she hardly recognized her two friends. Denny was wearing a well-cut suit of grey flannel and a stripy tie, and Peggy was wearing a skirt for once, and even a hat. "Coo-er!" said Maddy. "Sure you won't be ashamed to walk down to the station with me?"

As they waited for the train to start, they both assured her that they would see her soon, and once more she waved until her wrist ached as much as her heart. She walked slowly home dragging her feet.

"Something for you in the lounge," her mother told her. It was a lovely bunch of roses with a card which said, "For my favourite film star, remembering many headaches," and signed "Hans Van Velden."

Maddy ran to show her mother. "Look! Look!" she cried. "I've never been given flowers before!" She sniffed them rapturously. There was even an air of departure about her own house, for Sandra's luggage stood in the hall.

"Are you going down to the station to see Sandra off tomorrow?" her mother wanted to know.

"No!" said Maddy. "I'm sick of seeing people off. I wish I could be seen off for a change."

"Never mind!" said her mother. "Your time will come."

"I shall feel quite proud of myself when I get back," said Sandra comfortingly, "to be referred to as 'the sister of the film star'."

"Oh, by the way, Maddy, dear," said Mrs. Fayne. "I want you to come out with me this afternoon to buy you a new school hat and to see the dentist. We haven't long before your term begins, you know."

When Mrs. Fayne was ready to go out that afternoon she searched for Maddy, but there was no sign of her. Maddy was speeding towards Browcliffe on her bicycle. But even here she found no comfort, for every turn of the road reminded her of some remark of Rodney's or what Felicity had said just here…. And lying on her back on the cliff top she saw that the grass was not so green and the leaves were turning brown on the trees. The enchanted summer was over.

11

FAREWELL, LEICESTER SQUARE

Into the gloom of the autumn term came a letter from Van Velden. It was on an enormous sheet of thick notepaper, written in green ink in his sprawling hand.

"Dear little friend and big star," he wrote, "how are you getting? Here there is great exciting and busyness for the première of *Forsaken Crown*, a month from today at the Palaceum, Leicester Square. We look forward to see you, of course. Where will you stay? There are many peoples wishing to meet you. A big event it will be and may lead to who knows. Felicity gives afterwards a party and invites you. Write, please, and let me to hear of your arrangements. Yours of sincerity, Hans Van Velden."

Maddy gave a whoop of delight and showed it to her mother and father who were equally thrilled.

"Yes," said her father. "I think I shall have to take some time off and we'll go up for it, eh?"

"Oh, goody!" Maddy had not been so happy for weeks. "I'll wear all my new clothes – Oh, I'm longing for it. Where shall we stay?"

"Let me think," said her father. "I suppose it would have to be somewhere fairly decent. How about the 'Wiltshire'?"

"Can we afford it?" asked Mrs. Fayne dubiously.

"Of course," said Maddy. "I've got piles in the bank, haven't I? Denny Dent said so."

"Oh, we wouldn't dream of touching that, dear," said her mother.

"But why not? It's because of me you're going to London, so why not use some of my money? Then we can stay somewhere with lifts." This was Maddy's idea of luxury.

Finally her parents agreed to make it a real fling, and Mrs. Fayne bought a new coat for the occasion. Plans were made to meet Sandra and to see at her Dramatic School a show that all the Blue Doors were appearing in. Maddy talked of nothing else but the visit to London, and started to pack her case a week beforehand. One day the daily newspaper printed an advertisement for the film with a rather blurred photo of Maddy, Felicity, and Russell, and even stated the prices of the seats, which seemed to Maddy exorbitant.

"Gosh!" she said. "I wouldn't pay that just to see me!"

As Mrs. Potter-Smith walked down the High Street looking for someone with whom she might gossip she spied Miss Gaunt, Maddy's headmistress, striding along with her little attaché case. "Ah, Miss Gaunt! How nice to see you. And how are you?"

"Oh, very fit, Mrs. Potter-Smith, thank you. And how are you?"

"Just as busy a little person as ever, you know. And how is your dear school getting on?"

"Nearly at the end of term now and things are going pretty steadily."

Mrs. Potter-Smith registered surprise. "Really? In spite of all this excitement over that little Madelaine Fayne being a film star?"

"Oh, yes. She's a sensible child and doesn't put on airs. In fact she's very popular."

Mrs. Potter-Smith sighed. "I think you're wonderful, Miss Gaunt. I really do. How you manage a school with all the little girls running off to make films, I really don't know."

"Madelaine Fayne is the only one," demurred Miss Gaunt, "and it was only last term that she had a lot of time off. There was some talk of her going back to London with them for a few finishing-off details, but she didn't know anything about that. They applied to me and I put my foot down about it."

"And a good thing too," said Mrs. Potter-Smith. "Once these children start thinking they're important there's no holding them. Are you going up to town to see the première of this infant prodigy, by the way?"

"Oh, the première. And when is that?"

"Very soon, I believe. I wonder that you shouldn't know, because Mrs. Fayne was telling me the other day that she and her husband are going up with Maddy for the occasion. I should have thought she would have asked your permission to take Maddy away from school."

Miss Gaunt frowned. "Hm! Yes. That is rather funny. Well, it's been very nice to see you, Mrs. Potter-Smith. I must get along now."

"Yes, and so must I. Really one doesn't have a minute to spare for gossiping, does one? Good-bye, dear Miss Gaunt, and don't have too much trouble with our little film star, will you?"

The seeds of discontent were successfully sown in Miss Gaunt's mind. She went back to school with her lips set in a rather grim line.

That afternoon Maddy knocked at her door. "Please," she said, when she had been told to come in, "here's a note from my mother." Miss Gaunt read it quickly.

"Is it all right?" asked Maddy eagerly.

"Do pull up your left stocking, Madelaine," replied Miss Gaunt, then after a few seconds, "No, I'm afraid it's not all right. Your mother asks if you may be absent on the Thursday before the end of term. Now you know that exams will be on by then, don't you?"

"Yes," said Maddy, "but it's so important. It's the première, you see."

"The exams are equally important, Maddy!"

"Why? I shall probably fail most of them."

"You certainly will," her headmistress told her, "if you're in a rebellious mood."

"Well, I shall be if you don't let me go to the première, so why not let me go and put me down as failed. It won't worry me." Miss Gaunt looked angry.

"You're forgetting yourself, Maddy. How dare you speak to a mistress like that!" Maddy twisted the fringed edge of her girdle.

"But, Miss Gaunt, please stop being a schoolmistress for a moment and be a real person. I know you've been kind to me in the past to let me off school during the film, but even then I had a governess. But this is just as important, really it is. I've only been to London once before. For a day. We went to the Zoo and I ate all the monkey-nuts and felt ill, so really I've never seen London, and now there are lots of people Mr. Van Velden says I've got to meet for business purposes, and Felicity's having a party afterwards and everyone will be there, and I've got a new dress I've never worn – a red one. Oh, Miss Gaunt, please, please!"

Miss Gaunt sat like a piece of stone. "It's no good, Maddy. My mind is made up. Much as I should like you to go from a personal point of view, for the good of the school you must stay. People are already criticising my leniency towards you."

"People?"

"Yes. I met one of the Ladies' Institute who was most –"

"Mrs. Potter-Smith," shouted Maddy. "The old snake! I'd like to –"

"Maddy!" said Miss Gaunt sharply. "That's enough. You may tell your mother exactly what I have said."

Maddy looked at her in silence for a long time and then said quietly, "I warn you, Miss Gaunt. I am going to the première."

Miss Gaunt said equally quietly, "We shall see. You may go now. Oh, and just pull up that stocking again, will you?"

Maddy repeated this conversation to her mother and father that night, ending up, "But we're going all the same, aren't we?"

"Well," said her father, frowning, "I don't see how we can. If we took you away from school now that she has said you are not to go it would cause a lot of unpleasantness. No, I'm afraid it's entirely out of the question."

"Oh, *what* a pity!" said Mrs. Fayne. "I was so looking forward to it. Don't cry, dear. Perhaps we can go up later when your holidays begin. Couldn't we, Daddy?"

"Yes, we might do that."

"But it wouldn't be the same!" sobbed Maddy. "This is the première – and then there's the party. Oh, Miss Gaunt is beastly and all through that awful Potter-Smith. Why did you ever have to tell her, Mummy?"

"Oh dear! I'm sorry I did now. But she has that effect on me. I find her drawing all sort of things out of me that I never mean to tell her at all."

Maddy cried for the rest of the evening until her eyes were swollen and her nose was pink. Next morning, however, she was more cheerful. It seemed incredible that anyone could be so cruel as to stop her seeing the première of the film on which she had spent so much work and thought for so long. Something would turn up. It had got to. Every day she expected a summons to Miss Gaunt to hear that she had changed her mind, but it did not come. The day of the première found her sitting at her desk with an arithmetic paper in front of her. She sat and stared round the room, fuming. She had done the first two questions which were moderately easy, but now she was stumped. It was nearly four o'clock. In a few hours' time it would be starting. Sandra and Mr. Van Velden and Felicity and Rodney – they would all be sitting in the Palaceum in Leicester Square.

"I've never seen Leicester Square," she thought. " 'Goodbye Piccadilly, farewell Leicester Square.' There are lots of lights there. Perhaps my name is in lights outside the cinema. And here I sit working out impossible percentages."

Miss Gaunt's voice broke in upon her thoughts. "Now then, what are you dreaming about, Maddy?"

Maddy looked at her as much as to say, "Now what do *you* think I'm dreaming about?"

"I'm sorry, child!" she said more kindly. "But you really must get on with your work. It doesn't do to mope. That won't help things at all."

"H'm! *She's* sorry!" thought Maddy. "Oh, why can't I just jump out of the window and walk and walk. But I'd never get there in time. If I had a horse – a lovely black charger – I'd go galloping away. But I've only got a rather rattly bicycle."

An idea dawned slowly, it was so daring that she tried to push it out of her mind but it would not go. "If I started directly after school," she thought, "and rode ever so fast I might get there before the end, and that's the most important. Yes, I'll get to the party even if I miss the film." She wriggled in her chair with excitement. At last the hands of the clock moved round to four.

"Now then, girls," said Miss Gaunt. "Come along and give your papers in. Thank you, Maddy. Maddy, where are you going?" she cried, as Maddy raced to the door. "Come back! I haven't dismissed the class yet."

Maddy ran all the way home inflamed with her idea. She ran upstairs and drew the new red dress out of the wardrobe. It was woollen, but had short sleeves, and a white collar and white pockets. Hastily she put it on, her old school coat over the top, and ran down the stairs.

"Maddy!" said her mother. "Why have you got your new dress on, dear? You'll get it dirty."

"Oh, I just thought I'd wear it to cheer me up. I'm going to call on Lord Moulcester. I missed last week, so I'm going twice this week. He'll probably invite me to tea, so don't worry if I'm late. I'll take my bike, I think."

"All right, dear. Now, you're not fretting about the première, are you? Because Daddy says that we'll all go up in the Xmas holidays and we can stay a whole week."

"That will be nice. Well, cheerio!"

Mrs. Fayne remarked to her husband at tea, "I must say Maddy's taking it very well. She hasn't complained at all today."

"Good!" said Mr. Fayne. "I thought she'd soon get over it."

Maddy was out at Fennymead in record time. As she was passing the entrance to the castle drive, a car shot out. It was Lord Moulcester. Maddy pretended not to notice him and rode faster than ever. Lord Moulcester slowed down and turned to watch as she disappeared round the next bend. Then he went on to his meeting of the town council. Maddy sang little cheering tunes to herself and recited pieces of her speeches from the film. In a few hours she was to see it complete for the first time. She had of course seen herself on the screen when the "rushes" were being seen, but that was very different for they had only been little bits, and Van Velden had talked to her all the time.

"Yes, zat is goot. No. Zat we must do once more." How lovely to see everyone again! There was so much she wanted to say to them all. Pictures revolved in her brain as the white road stretched away in front of her. Van Velden saying, "Ach, so our little star is here –" Sandra crying, "Maddy! However did you get here?" Seeing the film. – A lovely party with lots to eat. –

"London!" said Maddy, "here I come!"

FORSAKEN CROWN

Sandra sat in the taxi on the very edge of the seat so that she would not crush the skirt of her evening dress. Although she had made it herself she was pretty sure that no one at the première would guess. It was a full black velvet skirt and a powder blue chiffon blouse with voluminous bishop sleeves. Over the top she wore the pièce de résistance – an ermine cloak borrowed from the kindly wardrobe mistress at her Dramatic School. She wore high-heeled black sandals belonging to Vicky and her thin-spun stockings were lent by Lynette. The rest of the Blue Doors were unable to afford seats for the première, so they were going in the cheaper seats next day. Nevertheless, they had given Sandra a magnificent send-off. Lynette and Vicky had swept her hair on to the top of her head and anchored it with many hair-pins. They had manicured her hands and supervised her make-up, while the boys looked on and made fatuous remarks. Bulldog went out and fetched a taxi for her, opened the door and saluted smartly as she stepped in, "Palaceum, Leicester Square!" he told the driver. The door banged, the five left standing on the pavement cheered, and the evening had begun.

Now that the lights of Leicester Square grew nearer, Sandra began to feel nervous. If only Maddy were here. She was always so un-self-conscious on occasions like this. And there in the distance flashed the sign *Forsaken Crown* over an illuminated coronet. Underneath, in smaller letters was "Madelaine Fayne". Sandra swelled with pride. How important it looked. Of course it would be a success. The taxi drew in to the kerb and the portly commissionaire opened the door. As she stepped out and paid the fare she was very conscious that the pavement was lined with sightseers, who were "star-spotting".

"Who's that?" she heard the murmur all round.

"It's Madelaine Fayne!" shouted someone.

"No, it ain't!"

"Yes, it is!" Sandra had never realized before that she bore any resemblance to Maddy. The crowd surged forward, peering at her eagerly. It seemed as if she would never reach the safety of the lighted foyer. Then she saw Denny Dent, looking very dashing in evening dress, pressing through the crowd towards her.

"Hullo, Sandra," he said. "I hardly recognized you."

"Is that Madelaine Fayne?" someone demanded.

"No," he told them. "Her sister."

There were disappointed noises from the crowd, but they still seemed interested as Sandra, on Denny Dent's arm, made her way into the foyer. Here all was warmth and colour. Evening dresses of every shade, men carrying silk hats, diamonds flashing – Sandra was almost overwhelmed. Wherever she turned she saw famous stage and film stars. And there was Van Velden, very pink in the face with excitement, trying to talk to a dozen people at once. He seemed to be bursting out of his shirt front. With him was Felicity in a white dress that took Sandra's breath away.

"Ach, Sandra, my child, welcome to you!" Van Velden clasped her hand in both his. "How sorry we are not to have your leetle sister with us tonight. But it is good you to see."

Felicity said, "Hullo, dear! Isn't this a crush. You do look lovely!"

There was a sudden blinding flash and Sandra jumped, "Don't worry. It's only the press cameras."

From somewhere Rodney appeared, lankier than ever in evening dress. He had not been able to make his tufty hair stay down despite applications of hair oil. His eyes were excited behind his spectacles. He and Sandra stood "star-spotting" while Van Velden made welcoming noises at all the people who mattered.

"Ach, what a dolt-head am I!" he said, turning to them. "I have just greeted ze Spanish ambassador in Dutch, and ze Dutch ambassador in Spanish!"

"I don't suppose they could hear you anyhow," roared Rodney above the noise.

Hans kept introducing Sandra to people whose names she could not hear and they could certainly not hear hers, but many of their faces she knew, and it was not till some minutes later that she would turn to Rodney and say, "Gosh! That must have been So-and-So."

Russell Durrant and Michael Strong arrived after much signing of autographs outside the doors. Everyone seemed to be there. Peggy was in fox furs, looking very unlike the efficient woman director in slacks that she appeared on the set. Even Miss Garrard, Maddy's governess, turned up in an incredible brown-lace dress and a flower in her crimped-for-the-occasion hair. At last it was time to go in. The cinema organ was playing, the sides of the proscenium were decorated with flowers. All was plush velvet and soft lighting. Sandra found herself seated between Rodney and Van Velden in the front row of the dress circle. Around them sat the rest of the cast and all the important people at the head of the firm, and also those under contract to the company. The lights dimmed. There was a Silly Symphony, the news, and a travel film to be endured first.

"I couldn't care less about bird life in California!" said Rodney. "Why don't they get on with the works?"

In the short interval Sandra noticed that Van Velden was constantly mopping his brow. "Don't worry!" she whispered. "It's going to be all right."

He made pathetic noises of prostration and said, "I wish that never I had come. Suppose they laugh in ze wrong places? Always before, my films have been comedy –"

Rodney too was getting nervous. "Of course," he kept saying. "No one will notice the music. They never do."

"Thank goodness," thought Sandra, "I don't have to be nervous on my own account. But oh, Maddy – they *must* like you." She reflected on how different it all was from the theatre. If this had been a play there would be hope that whatever it had been like in rehearsal, the thrill of a first night would give it life, but in this case the film was all safely "in the can", and nothing anyone did now could make it any better or worse. The public could take it or leave it.

At last the heavy velvet curtains swept back, and the certificate of the Board of Censors appeared. Sandra felt Rodney jump as the first slow bars of his music were heard. Then came a shot of Fennymead Castle with the title thrown across it, then the words "starring Madelaine Fayne, with Felicity Warren, Russell Durrant and Michael Strong. A Van Velden production". Then all the credits. Sandra could hardly sit still with excitement. Maddy did not appear until it had been running for about five minutes. When she did, swinging on the branch of an oak tree, a murmur of interest ran round the house.

"Doesn't she look a poppet!" said Rodney. "Oh! I wish she were here –"

"She's probably at home doing her homework," said Sandra.

The audience was very quiet and seemed to be reacting quite nicely. There were several laughs at Maddy's naïve lines and Felicity and Russell seemed to be getting away with the romantic sequences. Felicity watched herself on the screen rather doubtfully, shaking her head slowly at intervals. She turned to Rodney.

"Am I as ham as that on the stage?" she whispered.

"Don't know," he replied. "I've never seen you."

This seemed to them in their strung-up condition incredibly funny, and they giggled until one of the strong dramatic scenes between Maddy and Michael Strong.

"Never haf I seen a child to screen so well," said Van Velden to Sandra. "If we can thin her down a little as she grow up –" He did not finish the sentence.

In one of the pathetic scenes, the death of Maddy's little dog, there was a close-up of Maddy digging his grave, and Sandra noticed a flutter of white handkerchiefs below in the stalls and even an audible sniff.

"Which," said Rodney, "is pretty good for a première audience."

It seemed to go very quickly. Every detail was so familiar to them that it was like hearing an old bed-time story that had been so many times repeated as to be part of their lives. Then came the happy ending, Felicity and Russell, holding Maddy by the hand, running down a grassy slope and a final close-up of Maddy laughing. There was actually a burst of applause. Sandra turned to Van Velden as the lights went up.

"It was a success – wasn't it?" she asked.

"We do not know, my dear, not until the morning papers we see. We had reporters in ze house tonight and also they were this morning at a private Press showing."

"Let's go down into the foyer quickly," said Rodney after "The King" had been played, "and hear what people are saying."

They pushed their way down. Most people were saying, "Wasn't it good?" in rather surprised tones. "What a nice child!" "Wasn't she sweet?" "What did you say the little girl's name was?" Felicity was seized upon and congratulated by many friends, and once more Sandra was mistaken for Maddy. An earnest-looking elderly gentleman approached her and said, "Thank you, my dear, for a most moving performance." Sandra realized that he could hardly have picked her out from among the crowd of "vague villagers" so she said, "I'm afraid it wasn't me. It was my little sister."

"Really? Oh, I'm sorry! Yes, of course, you look older. But do congratulate her from me." He moved off.

Rodney said, "You're doing all right, aren't you?"

"What do you mean?"

"That was Sir Boris Bartov of N.D.N. Pictures."

"Phew!" said Sandra.

"If you'd fluttered your eyelashes a bit you might have got a contract."

Felicity was inviting everyone she knew to come to her party. Sandra wondered how they would all get into Felicity's tiny flat. Once more the Press cameras flashed, the diamonds glittered and the celebrities waiting for their cars on the steps pretended not to notice the goggling crowds on the pavements.

They all piled into cars and taxis to go to Felicity's. Sandra was in the back of Van Velden's car with at least half-a-dozen other people all saying how much they enjoyed the film. Someone said, "I heard the *Echo* film critic say, 'Now *there's* a screen child who doesn't make me want to crawl under the seat.' "

"How lovely!" cried Sandra.

They climbed the stairs to Felicity's flat. It was in a mews and very small, but tastefully decorated with gay curtains and cushions. Felicity had set out a pageant of sandwiches, savouries, and delicacies. There was a cocktail cabinet loaded with exciting things to drink. Everyone dumped their coats in the bedroom until there was nothing to be seen but mountains of fur and cloth.

"Come along!" said Felicity. "I'm afraid there's not much to eat, but do attack what there is. Hans, would you like to cope with the drinks?"

"Your vish is my command. And I must say a drink I haf need of. Neffer in my life haf I for three hours sat on bricks so hot."

"You needn't have done," Rodney told him. "It really was terrific. I've never seen a première audience so enthusiastic in my life."

"It is to our little Maddy we must drink," said Van Velden. "Come now! Your glasses you must fill and we shall drink toasts. Here is to our little Maddy, most budding young actress, who will conquer the hearts of millions with the toss of a pigtail." They all drank.

"Oh, I *do* wish she were here," said Felicity.

"And here is to the downfall of all headmistresses," went on Hans. "Let them be abolished." He proposed the toast of everyone in turn, and then they fell with vigour upon the sandwiches which disappeared like magic. There were many people there whom Sandra did not know, but they all talked to her and asked her questions about Maddy: "Is she really only twelve?" "Is her hair that colour naturally?" "Why isn't she here tonight?"

Sandra quite enjoyed her role of "sister of the star", especially when people told her that she too ought to be in films. Felicity introduced her to her agent, a little round, podgy man, as broad as he was long, who told her to call on him when she was ready to leave Dramatic School. Someone put on the radiogram, the rugs were rolled back, and there was dancing.

In the room there were various groups of people amusing themselves in different ways. Van Velden was telling funny stories in many languages to a group of people who were writhing with laughter. Rodney had found some music friends who were all humming tunes at each other in a corner and arguing violently. As Sandra danced with Denny Dent she thought it was the loveliest party she had ever been to. Catching sight of herself in a mirror she realized that not only did she look extremely grown-up, but quite as presentable as anyone there. The room revolved about them as they waltzed, and scraps of conversation came to her.

"And Mr. Smith, 'e look at ze dog and say, 'But mine dog was not all that shaggy...'"

"Yes, but don't you think that with Beethoven it's a different matter –"

"I can't forget that shot of the castle reflected in the moat –"

The shrill call of the telephone was hardly heard above the din. Felicity answered it.

"Hullo! Yes, this is Mayfair 59753. A trunk call? Yes, I'll hold on." She raised her voice above the noise. "Do you mind being quiet just one minute, folks," Instantly silence fell and everyone listened. "Fayne? Yes. Hold on, please. Sandra, it's for you."

Sandra had felt a sense of foreboding as soon as the bell had rung. "For me?" She ran to the phone. From far away her mother's voice came faintly and Sandra could tell she was worried.

"Is that you, Sandra? Maddy's missing. She went out after school and she hasn't been back. She said she was going to see Lord Moulcester, but I've rung him over and over again and he's not in. Daddy's been down to the castle but there's no one there. You've not heard anything of her?"

"No," said Sandra, "but I'll let you know the minute I do."

"Daddy's gone to the police station now."

Sandra tried to comfort her mother and then rang off. When she turned to the rest of the party who were listening in silence, her face was very white. "Maddy's run away," she said.

13

LONDON ROAD

It began to get cooler and the roads were not so familiar. Maddy wished that she had a lamp on her bicycle as dusk turned into darkness. There was a moon, but it was so often behind the clouds. Her legs ached with pedalling and the saddle seemed to get harder and harder. In the distance flashed a sign saying "Café" and she had suddenly realized that she was hungry. Outside the café a lot of lorries were parked. She left her bicycle and opened the door. A smell came out and hit her – a smell of bacon frying, and tomatoes and onions and chips. Her mouth watered. She looked round at the little wooden tables, where men were eating from fantastically piled plates, crouched low over them, their eyes fierce with concentration. The air was smoky from many Woodbines. Behind the counter a cheerful-looking woman with a scarlet face was ladling the steaming food out of bubbling lakes of fat. She looked at Maddy with surprise.

"Hullo!" said Maddy. "I've only got ninepence, so would you give me some of whatever is most filling, please."

The woman heaped up a plate with egg, bacon, and beans and poured an enormous cup of tea that was so strong it was nearly black. Maddy carried it to a table and attacked it thankfully.

When she had washed the meal down with the tea she felt better and sat up and looked around. It was a shock to find that the clock hands pointed to nine. What hours she had been cycling! She looked at the comic strips in several newspapers that were lying around and listened to the conversations of football and dog racing. She was pleasantly sleepy. If she were at home she would be in bed – For a few minutes she had forgotten the object of her journey, but with a flash she remembered the lights of Leicester Square and jumped up calling, "Good-night" to the lady behind the counter. Outside it seemed darker and cooler and more unfriendly than before her meal. She got on her bicycle and sped forward. The only sound that broke the silence of the countryside was the tinkling of her bell as she swept round the bends in the road.

When the meeting of the town council was over Lord Moulcester happened to walk down the stairs of the town hall with Miss Gaunt. "We are all so glad," she said, "that you are taking part in the local activities so much more nowadays, Lord Moulcester. We always used to think of you as quite a hermit."

"It is a great surprise for me to find that I *can* join in with things again," said Lord Moulcester, "and I must say I enjoy it immensely. It has only happened since I became interested in the Fennymead film."

"Why, yes, of course," said Miss Gaunt. "I hadn't realized that."

"And that was all brought about by your little pupil, Madelaine."

"Really?" Miss Gaunt said with interest. "An odd child. I'm afraid she's very upset at the moment because I wouldn't allow her time off to go up to London for the première."

"That's today, isn't it?" said Lord Moulcester.

"Yes. Why aren't you attending it?"

"I was invited, but I have a strong dislike for London."

"Poor Maddy! She was so bad-tempered all day today. She went out of the classroom like a whirlwind at four o'clock."

"Yes," remarked Lord Moulcester. "I saw her out cycling for all she was worth this evening."

"Where?" asked Miss Gaunt alarmed.

"Oh, out along the London road," was the casual reply.

"The London road!" cried Miss Gaunt.

"Yes – oh, good heavens!"

Lord Moulcester suddenly realized her train of thought. "Of course. She would do something like that."

"What time did you see her?"

"About five."

"And she'd got out to Fennymead? She warned me that she intended to go to the première – It's about nine now, so she's had four hours' start. What ought we to do?" asked Miss Gaunt anxiously. "Inform the police or her parents?"

"Neither!" said Lord Moulcester. "We'll follow her in my car. It's outside. Come along. We've no time to lose. If we can get her back tonight we shall save her parents a lot of anxiety."

"But suppose she's nearer London than Fenchester by the time we reach her?" demurred Miss Gaunt.

"In that case," said Lord Moulcester. "I shall have to forget my dislike of London." He opened the car door. "Get in, Miss Gaunt."

Maddy's legs felt like lead. It was lovely to rest them when she went downhill, but on the other side there was always another hill to go up. She came to some crossroads. She couldn't quite see the signpost, but she chose the biggest road and struggled on.

"If only I could have another rest," she thought, "but I mustn't yet. It's after ten. I expect I've missed the film. But I must, I must get to the party."

There was a cold wind blowing against her and the road seemed never-ending. It unrolled in front of her continuously, with no sign at all of London. She was riding almost in a dream when there was an ominous pop and a hissing noise. The bicycle began to jerk and bump like a live thing.

"No!" Maddy said aloud. "It *can't* be a puncture. It mustn't be." But it was. She tried to ignore it and ride on, but the bumping was too much. She got off and laid the bike on the grass at the side of the road. "I'll rest for a very little while," she thought, "and decide what to do next." The grass, though cold, seemed soft, and she stretched herself out luxuriously. "I must keep awake," she thought, "because of London," but the next moment she was in a deep sleep of fatigue.

Lord Moulcester drove fast with his headlights full on. "I'm afraid we may miss her, Miss Gaunt. It's getting so dark."

"We must find her now," said Miss Gaunt. "I can't imagine how she's managed to get so far."

"Once Maddy makes up her mind about something it's amazing how she achieves it," Lord Moulcester remarked.

"Do you know where she is likely to go if she gets as far as London?" asked Miss Gaunt. "The film will obviously be over by that time."

"Yes, I'm pretty sure she'll make for Felicity Warren's place. She is having a party tonight, and she sent me an invitation, so I have the address."

"I feel rather guilty at not giving her permission to go in the first place," said Miss Gaunt.

"And why didn't you?"

"Frankly, it was all the fault of that old Mrs. Potter-Smith. I met her in the town and she threw out hints that people were criticizing my treatment of Maddy, which annoyed me somewhat."

"That woman causes most of the trouble in Fenchester," said Lord Moulcester bitterly. "I should like to see her deported."

"Poor little Maddy. She may have lost her way by this time. Oh, I do hope she hasn't been kidnapped or anything," said Miss Gaunt. "I should feel it was all my fault."

Lord Moulcester chuckled. "Anyone kidnapping Maddy would very soon return her, I'm sure."

"All the same, I'm worried."

They drove on in the silence of the night that held no trace of Maddy.

The sound of a lorry approaching woke Maddy. She sat up and rubbed her legs which were stiff with cold. For a minute she could not remember what she was doing on the edge of the road at this time of night. Then she remembered. A puncture, of course – The lorry roared nearer and she leaped to her feet. She *must* get a lift to London. As it turned the corner she stepped into the glare of its lights and waved her arms.

"Hi! Stop!" she yelled. "Stop!" There was a squeal of brakes and mutterings from the driver as the lorry came to a standstill. Then a head was poked out of the window.

"Well I'll be – if it ain't a nipper!" said a kind sort of voice. "Wot you doin' this hour o' the night?"

"I'm on my way to London and my bike has got a puncture. I wonder if you could give me a lift?"

"Well, you're a cool one, you are. 'Course I'd give you a lift, but I've just come *from* London. Yore on the wrong road, ducks."

Maddy gasped. "Oh no! I can't be! Oh dear! I'll miss the party now."

"Going to a party, eh? Sure you're not runnin' away from home?"

"No, of course not!" said Maddy indignantly "Look, I've got my new party dress on."

The lorry driver seemed dubious. "I dunno as 'ow I ought-n'ter turn you over to a copper. What'll yer Ma be thinkin', eh?"

"She'll soon guess where I've gone. But if you're going in the wrong direction it's no good, is it? I'll have to leave my bike and walk back to wherever I went wrong."

"Look 'ere, me girl," put in the lorry driver. "It's past midnight. I can't leave you roamin' around like a bloomin' babe in the wood. Tell you wot – I'm goin' back to London eventually about four or five this mornin'. Gotter go and pick up a load o' cabbages to take back to Covent Garden, so you can come alonger me if you like. Better'n freezin' on the road all night without gettin' a hitch."

"That's very kind of you," said Maddy, "but I did want to be in time for the party."

"Cheer up, Dinah," said the man comfortingly. "P'raps it'll still be on by the time you gets there. You know what parties are."

Maddy cheered up. "Yes! I expect it will still be on. O.K., Mr. Lorry Driver. I'll come and collect cabbages with you."

"Jump in, then!" He opened the door for her and then went round and put her bike in the back, and jumped in again. The engine roared and they were off. It was terribly exciting. The headlights made the road immediately in front of them as bright as day and little rabbits scurried nervously about to escape.

"I've never ridden in a lorry before," shouted Maddy above the noise of the engine. "Gosh! This is better than my bicycle."

"Look 'ere," said the lorry driver, "what I still can't make out is why a brat like you is tryin' to get to a party in London at this time o' night anyway. Where've you come from?"

"Fenchester."

"Well, I'll be – And cycled all the way?"

"Yes. Until I had a puncture about an hour ago."

The man peered at her. "There's something about that clock o' yours wot strikes me as familiar-like," he said slowly. "You aven't 'ad yer pitcher in the paper as missin' from 'ome, 'ave yer? Wot's yer name?"

"You may have seen my photo," Maddy told him, "but not because I'm missing. My name is Madelaine Fayne."

He repeated it. "Madelaine Fayne. Don't mean nothing to me – Hey! Wait a minute. Are you tellin' me yore Madelaine Fayne? That new film star wot just made a film about some 'istorical stuff?"

"Yes, that's right."

"Garn!" he said disbelievingly.

"It's quite true. Of course you don't have to believe me."

"Kind of you, I'm sure. Now, come on, kid! Open up. Let's 'ear the truth." He shone a torch on her face. "Well, I'll be blowed! I believe you *are* 'er. Seen a photo in the *Movie World*, I did." He seemed quite awed. "Well, this is the first time I've 'ad a film star in this van. Beg yer parding, Miss, fer not believin' yer."

"Oh, for heaven's sake don't call me Miss. I'm Maddy."

"And I'd be glad if you'd call me Bert."

"O.K., Bert! Where do we have to go to collect the cabbages?"

"Not so far now. We'll be back in the Garden about five. Better make yourself cushy. 'Ere y'are. There's some sackin' behind the seat."

Maddy wrapped it about her. "Oh, this is fun. I'm so glad I met you, Bert."

"It ain't s'dusty fer me either. Gets a bit lonely, yer know, all on yer ownsome with nothin' but the road goin' on and on in front of yer all the bloomin' time."

"I bet it does." After a while he began to sing in a lusty bass, and Maddy joined in:

> "Daisy, Daisy,
> Gimme yer answer, do –"

The lorry ate up the miles.

The night wore on. Miss Gaunt said to Lord Moulcester, "Poor child! She may be shivering by the road-side somewhere."

"So I says to 'im," Bert continued the long story. "So you don't like the look of me, eh? Well, I can't say as 'ow I'm all that taken with yore bloomin' mug, either, see? Well, I could see he was gettin' nasty, so what do you think I did, eh?"

The only reply was a slight snore from Maddy, who, curled up in her corner, dreamed of the lights of London.

14

ANOTHER PREMIÈRE

Rodney put a new record on the radiogram. The party had quietened down now to a gentle buzz of voices, with sometimes silence for a few minutes. Most of the guests had gone home – only a few stalwarts remained, waiting for the morning papers and to see if Maddy would turn up. Sandra, sitting on a cushion on the floor, was ashamed to have to admit that she was still enjoying herself. Of course, the news that Maddy was missing had shaken her, but everyone assured her that she was certain to turn up before long. And now the firelight, the music, and the soothing conversation were wrapping her in a web of contentment. As the night wore on people began to smoke more, and to make renewed attacks upon the sandwiches. Some people were unashamedly asleep, and even Van Velden would stop talking and doze for a few minutes, only to wake up, having remembered another funny story. As a change from the radiogram, Rodney played on the piano soft dreamy airs that suited the drowsy atmosphere. Sandra felt as if she had sat on her cushion for hours and as if she would never move from it again.

Lord Moulcester and Miss Gaunt lost a lot of time by following a false trail. An A.A. man at a box at the crossroads told them that a little girl on a bicycle had passed him some hours before and had taken, not the London road, but another turning. They drove down this road for a long time until Lord Moulcester said, "She can't possibly have got any farther along here or we should have overtaken her."

"Perhaps we had better turn back on to the London road," said Miss Gaunt. "I'm pretty sure now that we shan't find her anywhere but in or near London." So they retraced their tracks and made for London again.

"I apologize," said Lord Moulcester, "for letting you in for this long journey, Miss Gaunt. But at first I was certain that we should catch up with her after a very little while."

"That's quite all right," replied Miss Gaunt, and opened her mouth to say that she was enjoying herself, then decided not to.

Soon they were in the outskirts of London, and accelerated along the empty roads.

"If we don't find her," remarked Miss Gaunt, "we shall look rather silly."

"Whether we find her or not," asserted Lord Moulcester, "I intend to have a very large breakfast."

Miss Gaunt agreed that she, too, was hungry, and for the next few miles they discussed what they should have for their breakfast.

"'Ere we are!" said Bert. "Just gettin' into the old smoke. Where d'you want, eh? I'll dump you first then the cabbages. 'Ow's that?"

Maddy woke up for long enough to tell him the address of Felicity's flat.

"Coo! Posh, eh? Mayfair –" but Maddy was asleep again. The heavy lorry lumbered through the sleeping streets. When it reached the mews it was too large to go down the narrow turning so Bert drew in to the kerb and stopped. Behind him a motor-horn honked. As he got out he saw behind him a large limousine trying to turn down into the mews. "Shan't be a mo!" he shouted to the driver. "Just gotter deliver something." He went round and opened the door. Maddy was still fast asleep so he lifted her out in his arms and carried her towards the entrance to the flats.

"I say! Wait a minute!" a voice came from the limousine. A bearded man got out and faced Bert fiercely. "Where did you find that child?" he wanted to know.

Miss Gaunt stepped out and joined them. "He's kidnapped her! He's kidnapped her!" she cried, sleepy and rather hysterical after the all-night drive.

"I don't know who you are," said Bert, "and I don't care. All I know is I'm leavin' this kid at this address and then goin' back to deliver me cabbages." He turned his back on them and climbed the stairs to Felicity's flat.

Rodney was playing the Moonlight Sonata, the fire was burning low, and Denny Dent was reciting limericks to any of the company who happened to be awake, when the door bell pealed. Sandra leaped to her feet and Felicity ran to the door. There stood a funny little man in a cloth cap with a wooffly moustache. In his arms was Maddy, sleeping with a cherubic grin on her face.

"Maddy!" cried Felicity. Everyone crowded to the door. "But who on earth are you and wherever did you find her?"

There were footsteps on the stairs and Lord Moulcester and Miss Gaunt appeared, both talking very loudly at once.

Sandra thought that she must be delirious. "Lord Moulcester! Miss Gaunt! Whatever are you doing here?"

Everyone tried to talk at once. Bert carried Maddy into the room and laid her on the sofa. While they all crowded round her he stood on the edge of the group respectfully holding his cap in his hands. Then as no one took any more notice of him, he slipped away to his lorry, left Maddy's bicycle outside on the kerb, and departed to deliver his cabbages as methodically as he had delivered his first load.

"Is she all right?"

"Lord Moulcester, Miss Gaunt, have a drink. But how did you – Oh, this is too much."

All the people who did not know Maddy crowded to have a look at her. "Isn't she sweet!" "Poor little thing!"

"Doesn't she look angelic," said Rodney. "Oughtn't we to wake her and tell her what a success the film was? And I'm pretty sure she's hungry."

"No, don't wake her," said Sandra sharply.

But Maddy was already stretching and yawning. She opened her eyes. "What a lot of people. Is it still the party? Where's Bert?" They looked around for Bert but he had gone.

"Oh, what a pity!" said Felicity. "We ought to have given him a drink."

"And I never said 'thank you!'" Maddy rubbed her eyes and looked round the room. "Ow!" she squealed. "Miss Gaunt! And Lord Moulcester!"

"Yes!" said Miss Gaunt rather grimly. "Lord Moulcester and I followed you here in his car, you troublesome child."

"You didn't catch me, did you?" said Maddy complacently. "Oh! How was the film. All right?"

"All right?" cried Van Velden. "It was terrific. You will be an overnight riot, my little chicken. Now we wait for ze papers –"

"Oh, I *did* want to see it," said Maddy. "What a pity I had to go and collect cabbages first."

Felicity shook her head in despair. "I still fail to understand just how everyone got here, but I'm glad to see them all the same. Now I think I'll go and cook some bacon and eggs and we'll all have breakfast."

"Yum yum!" said Maddy. "Just what I need," and Lord Moulcester and Miss Gaunt cheered up a bit.

While breakfast was cooking Sandra rang up her parents to tell them that Maddy was safe, and they had a few words with Maddy over the phone, but were so relieved at hearing her voice again that they realized when they had rung off that they had forgotten to scold her.

Over the bacon and eggs a fuller account was given of the two pilgrimages, and everyone seemed to wake up thoroughly and laugh a lot. They all said what a shame it was that Maddy had not arrived in time for the film. Suddenly Rodney waved his knife and fork in the air.

"Listen! Listen, everyone!" he cried. "I've got an idea. I know the boy who operates the films at the Palaceum. He doesn't live far from here. Suppose I go round and knock him up and persuade him to show the film through for us, now – Another première, especially for Maddy and Miss Gaunt and Lord Moulcester."

It was a crazy idea, but it sounded attractive.

"Maddy's too tired!" objected Sandra.

"No, I'm not! No, I'm not!" cried Maddy. "Oh, do let's –"

Rodney leaped up and flung on his coat. "I'll ring you when it's all fixed," and he disappeared.

Felicity insisted that Maddy should have a hot bath, and that Lord Moulcester and Miss Gaunt should try to get some sleep. About six o'clock the phone rang.

"We're at the Palaceum!" said Rodney. "Come at once. We've bribed the night watchman, and there's a little door at the side unlocked."

It was still dark when they piled into Van Velden's car.

"This," said he, "is ze first time I go to two premières in twelve hours."

"What a crazy night!" said Sandra.

"I think it's been fun," said Maddy, for her long sleep on the lorry had refreshed her, so that she was perkier than anyone.

Rodney was waiting at the side door of the Palaceum. They went in rather stealthily, although they knew that if there were any trouble Van Velden could probably fix it. The stalls were draped in dust sheets, and only one working light was on. They sat in the middle of the stalls.

"O.K., Johnny!" shouted Rodney. "Let's have it."

Maddy thought to herself that this was even nicer than a real première – to have one all for her own benefit, and at six o'clock in the morning. After the first shock of seeing herself on the screen, which she always experienced even after having seen many "rushes" of the film, she quite enjoyed it, and even laughed loudly at a funny bit, and this made everyone else laugh too. Lord Moulcester was so charmed with his castle's appearance that he quite forgot his prejudice against the cinema, and even Miss Gaunt admitted that she was glad she had come. All who had been to the party showed a tendency to go to sleep, but Rodney's music woke them whenever a climax was reached.

"Van Velden has something which only continental directors can bring off," was Miss Gaunt's verdict. "He makes you laugh and cry at the same time."

At the end of it when the curtains had swung to, Van Velden shouted, "I call three cheers for Johnny, the operator!"

Johnny, the operator, came down and they all thanked him and gave him cigarettes, and he said what a good film it was.

"I'm hungry again," said Maddy. "Premières take it out of you. Where can we have some more breakfast?"

"Lyons!" said Rodney. "Let's go!"

They left the cinema in darkness again, "and no harm done," as Johnny, the operator, said. Outside it was light and people were scurrying to work.

"Of course," said Maddy, "it's tomorrow morning."

They made for Piccadilly in a straggling crocodile consisting of Rodney, Van Velden, and Denny in evening suits, Sandra and Felicity and Peggy in trailing frocks, Lord Moulcester, Miss Gaunt, and Maddy somewhat travel-worn, and Johnny, the operator, in dungarees. Suddenly Maddy stopped and laughed out loud.

"What's the matter?" asked Miss Gaunt.

"You wouldn't let *me* go to the première," laughed Maddy, "and now you've been yourself."

MORNING PAPERS

Outside the Piccadilly Corner House an old woman was selling papers. They had almost passed her when Rodney realized and shouted, "Papers –" Immediately they all besieged her and bought as many different ones as possible. They tried to open them there and then, but the morning wind blew too gustily and they had to give it up.

"Wait till we get inside," said Sandra.

Inside it was warm and marble-and-chromium, and smelt of coffee. A rather bewildered door-man opened the door of the restaurant. But he was used to seeing extraordinary groups of people at this hour of the morning. They hurried inside and sat down at two tables pushed together, as one was not big enough. A waitress hovered but they took no notice of her so she went away. Armfuls of papers were dumped on the table, and they turned the pages much too hurriedly to find anything. Rodney was the first.

"Here we are!" he cried. " 'New Child Star – Madelaine Fayne Makes Hit –' "

"Here's another," shouted Felicity, " 'Van Velden does it again – Child Discovery –' "

Sandra yelled, " '*Forsaken Crown* Première a Success. New Star Acclaimed –' "

Without exception the criticisms were favourable. Van Velden could not understand it.

"Ze *Echo* –" he said. "Read to me what Williamson of ze *Echo* say – Alvays he insult my work –"

They juggled with newspapers, upsetting the pepper and salt on the table to find the column in the *Echo*.

"This is the best yet of Van Velden's productions," it read, "and little Miss Madelaine Fayne is an actress of no mean talent. Between them they have given us the most outstanding British film of the year."

Van Velden embraced Maddy. "You see?" he said. "You see? I tell you it will be all right." Maddy was so thrilled she could hardly speak, yet inside her she had a peculiar feeling that these press notices could not be referring to her at all. "It is necessary," said Van Velden, "that you promise me not to sign nothing until you hear from our company, yes?"

"I'm afraid," said Miss Gaunt, "that Maddy won't be making any more films yet. I know that her parents are going to insist that she settles down now to work with her School Certificate in view."

"How like a schoolmistress!" thought Maddy, "to mention School Certificate at a moment like this." Her joy almost evaporated.

"Well, I have some news for Maddy that no one has heard yet," said Sandra with a gleam in her eye that made Maddy feel it was going to be nice news.

"My Dramatic School is opening a junior department next term for pupils of about Maddy's age, and it will have general education laid on, and I expect Mummy and Daddy will let her come. So you'll be relieved of the burden, Miss Gaunt."

Everyone laughed, and Miss Gaunt did not know whether to look glad or sorry. Maddy wore such a wide grin that Rodney told her it would meet and tie at the back if she were not careful. She felt so happy she was afraid she might burst. At last the waitress claimed their attention, and they ordered coffee and toast and marmalade. The people at the surrounding tables were regarding them curiously. What on earth did they think they were doing? All those newspapers and so much noise and evening clothes at this hour of the day! They drained their coffee and smoked more cigarettes, unwilling to break up the party. Johnny, the operator, was the first to leave.

"What's everyone doing?" Felicity wanted to know.

"I must get back to Fenchester," said Miss Gaunt firmly, "and Maddy must come too."

"But you can't possibly drive back all that way after no sleep last night," said Felicity to Lord Moulcester.

"I think you ought to have a rest," said Maddy.

"Why, what do you want to do?" Sandra asked.

"Explore!" said Maddy.

"Well, someone will have to go with you. We don't want to lose you again. And I must be getting along in a minute. We've got mime at ten o'clock and I must go back to the digs and change."

"I'll look after her," said Rodney.

Van Velden looked at his watch. "Goot heffings! I must to the studios get down."

Felicity said, "I suggest that Miss Gaunt and Lord Moulcester go back to the flat and get some rest. I've got a rehearsal at ten, but I'll be back about twelve and I'll cook you and Maddy an early lunch and you can get back this afternoon. How's that?"

This was agreed upon. They folded up their newspapers and Van Velden left the waitress an enormous tip to make up for all the noise. They parted outside, Maddy and Rodney saying good-bye to Sandra and Van Velden and Peggy. Everyone said it was the most exciting night they had ever spent. Van Velden took Lord Moulcester and Miss Gaunt back with Felicity in a taxi.

"Well," said Rodney, "you've got one morning in which to see London. Where do you want to go?"

Maddy thought of the Zoo, Westminster Abbey, Madame Tussaud's – oh, there were hundreds of things she ought to see. Finally she said, "Let's just walk."

"Where?" asked Rodney.

"Wherever looks interesting."

"O.K. Lead and I follow."

They walked and walked, stopping to look in shops and to have a little refreshment now and then. They went a little way by tube because Maddy loved escalators, and a little way by bus because she liked the tops of buses. They walked down Shaftesbury Avenue and St. Martin's Lane to look at the theatres, and Maddy tried to make up her mind which she would like to appear in first. They stopped at Felicity's theatre and looked at the photos of her that were hung outside.

"One day," said Maddy, "my photo's going to be here."

"Aren't you satisfied," said Rodney, "with having it plastered over the papers?"

"Oh, but that's only because of the film," said Maddy.

"You are a funny child. Are you still set on the stage when you've had such a good start in films?"

"Of course," said Maddy. "I'm going to Dramatic School next term. Yippee!"

"But even then you might go into films when you leave there."

"Bet I don't," said Maddy.

"Bet you do."

"Bet I don't."

"Bet you do."

This continued fruitlessly all the way down Charing Cross Road, then Maddy decided that she ought to take her mother a present.

"I should think so too!" said Rodney. "A pretty big one after all the worry you've given her."

They went into an antique shop and after burrowing among the cobwebs Maddy decided on a little Chinese god a few inches high.

"He's very ugly," she said, "but rather sweet."

They walked down to Trafalgar Square and bought some buns with which to feed the pigeons. Although the birds flocked round with the sunlight making their feathers glint silver, they did not get a lot of the buns from Maddy. It was a clear frosty winter day, but the sun was warm and the air invigorating. Maddy was thrilled with everything ... the traffic, the shops, the pigeons. And to think that next term she might be working in this wonderful city at last. She skipped along by Rodney's side, taking two steps to his one. Soon they were down on the Embankment. The tide was lapping against the banks below the Houses of Parliament. Little tugs chuffed importantly up and down, and people scurried along looking busy. Maddy and Rodney seemed to be the only ones idling pleasantly in a world of bustle. The attraction of the water was too much, and they leaned up against the parapet and watched.

"Aren't you tired?" asked Rodney, "after all your adventures?"

"No," said Maddy. "I'm ready for some more now." She

was in the exhilarated mood that comes after a very little sleep and too much excitement, but she knew that later in the day she would suffer for it.

"How do you feel about going back to school?"

"Oh, that –" said Maddy. "I don't mind a bit. There's only a little bit of this term left, then there's Christmas, and then I shall be going to Dramatic School. Oh, what a lucky girl I am!"

"You certainly are," said Rodney. "I bet you're the most envied child in England."

"I certainly wouldn't change with anyone else today," beamed Maddy. She stared at a tug on the river, "But I would rather like to be the man who drives one of those little boats. I've really got you to thank over the film," she went on, "because if you hadn't taken me down to the location it would never have all started."

"Don't be silly!" said Rodney. "If you hadn't been good enough you wouldn't have got any further than the test."

Maddy frowned. "But if the Bishop had never taken me for that walk over the Fennymead fields I shouldn't have known that Elizabeth was only a little girl, and Felicity would have kept the part."

"And it was only because you were naughty that the Bishop took you out," Rodney reminded her.

"But I shouldn't have been naughty if it hadn't been for that awful arithmetic all about Mr. A, and Mr. B, and Mr. C."

"Then it is to Mr. A., Mr. B., and Mr. C. that you attribute your fame, Miss Fayne," he said, apeing the reporters. "And what do you think of our London policemen?"

"I love everything about London," said Maddy solemnly. "Everything." She looked at it all. The traffic roared by, the river flowed on, the tugs chugged, a few sea-gulls screamed, Big Ben struck twelve, and all the time the people – hundreds of them – hurried everywhere.

"We must be going," said Rodney, but they did not move.

A little man in a bowler hat bought a newspaper and propped himself against the parapet beside them. He scanned the front page, passing over the photo of Maddy, then turned to the sporting page and settled down to read about the football.

And although Rodney was still telling her how good the film was and how famous she would be, Maddy realized for the first time exactly how small was her part in the scheme of things.